Wildflower Girl

When she was only seven, Peggy made a terrifying journey, with her sister Eily and brother Michael, through famine-torn Ireland. Now she sets out on another dangerous and frightening journey – to America. Crossing the Atlantic takes six long, uncomfortable weeks. What will Peggy find when she gets to the New World? And will she ever see her homeland and her beloved sister and brother again?

'As gripping a story as the original, embracing not just a sense of place – Ireland – but a sense of time and history. Conlon-McKenna has crafted this book ... not a word, spoken or unspoken, nor an emotion, is wasted. Pace and style keep the pages turning, and you are filled with a sense of wanting more at the end. Highly recommended'

Books Ireland

'The same good strong writing as is evidenced in *Under the Hawthorn Tree*'

The Sunday Tribune

WINNER
Historical Novel Category

Special Merit Award to The O'Brien Press
from Reading Association of Ireland
'for exceptional care, skill and professionalism in publishing, resulting in a consistently high standard in all of the children's books published by The O'Brien Press'

MARITA CONLON-McKENNA is one of Ireland's most popular children's authors. She has written many bestselling children's books. *Under the Hawthorn Tree*, her first novel, became an immediate bestseller and has been described as 'the biggest success story in children's historical fiction.' It has been reprinted numerous times since its first publication in 1990, and has reached a worldwide audience through translations and foreign editions. Its sequels, *Wildflower Girl* and *Fields of Home*, which complete the CHILDREN OF THE FAMINE trilogy, have also been hugely successful. Marita's other children's novels (see inside back cover) have also received wide critical acclaim.

DONALD TESKEY drew the chapter-head illustrations. His paintings have been exhibited to great acclaim in Europe and North America.

Other books by
MARITA CONLON-McKENNA

Under the Hawthorn Tree
Fields of Home
The Blue Horse
No Goodbye
Safe Harbour
In Deep Dark Wood
A Girl Called Blue

MARITA
CONLON-McKENNA
Wildflower Girl

Illustrated by Donald Teskey

THE O'BRIEN PRESS

DUBLIN

First published 1991 by The O'Brien Press Ltd,
12 Terenure Road East, Rathgar, Dublin 6, D06 HD27, Ireland.
Tel: +353 1 4923333; Fax: +353 1 4922777
E-mail: books@obrien.ie; Website: www.obrien.ie
Reprinted 1991. First paperback edition 1992.
Reprinted 1992, 1994, 1995, 1997, 1998,
1999, 2000 (twice), 2001, 2002, 2003, 2004, 2005, 2007 (twice),
2008, 2009, 2010 (twice), 2012, 2013, 2015, 2017.

ISBN 978-0-86278-283-2

26 28 29 27
17 19 21 20 18

Typesetting, editing, design, layout: The O'Brien Press Ltd
Internal illustrations: Donald Teskey
Cover illustration: PJ Lynch
Printed and bound by CPI Group (UK) Ltd, Croydon, CR0 4YY
The paper in this book is produced using pulp from managed forests.

The O'Brien Press receives assistance from

For all those who have sailed across
stormy seas to find a new life

Acknowledgements

I would like to thank my husband James, and
my children Amanda, Laura, Fiona and James
for their love and encouragement.
Thank you too to my family and friends,
to my sister-in-law Brigid Brady, to my
publisher The O'Brien Press, especially
Michael O'Brien, and to my wonderful
editor and good friend Ide ní Laoghaire,
and to Marilyn Malin in London.

I wish to thank the Arts Council and Aer Lingus,
the Ulster/American Folk Park, Phil Bergin at the Bostonian
Society, Lolly Sharp at
the Gibson House, Beacon Street Boston.
Thank you to all the librarians who have helped
me along the way: my local library in Stillorgan,
the National Library of Ireland, Trinity College Library,
the American Embassy Library, Dublin, Pearse Street
Library, Dublin, Cobh Library, Co. Cork,
Tim Cadogan at Cork City Library,
and Boston Public Library.

Contents

CHAPTER 1

The Bridge

 PEGGY RAN IN FROM SCHOOL and straight away she noticed the large sheet of paper propped behind a jug on the kitchen dresser. She grabbed it.

'I don't believe it! I just don't believe it! We got a notice about going to America too. A few in school told me their families had got them. The whole town's talking about it.' She was bursting with excitement.

Eily looked across at her.

'Whisht, Peggy! Take it easy.'

Eily's hands and arms were dusty to the elbows with flour. She was busy kneading dough to make bread.

'Eily, aren't you excited? How can you stand there baking bread when our whole future might depend on this bit of paper?'

Peggy looked across the kitchen. Her big sister was staring into the bowl on the scrubbed wooden table and refused to meet her eyes.

'There's something up! That's it! You're hiding something from me.'

The older girl stopped. With the back of her hand

she pushed a loose bit of fair hair aside, then shrugged.

'We're not going.'

'Eily, stop codding me. I'm not a fool!' shouted Peggy. Eily shook her head.

'No, I'm being serious, Peggy. Things have changed,' she said. 'So many things are different now,' she added in a low whisper.

'Changed!' shouted Peggy. 'Even I know they've changed. We've less money than ever. Some days we don't even get one customer in the shop and none of us can get a job. There's even more reason for us to go now.'

'Listen, Peggy, I told you! We're not going away. We're not leaving Castletaggart and that's all there is to it!'

'We … We … There are three of us. Why should you always be the one to decide for us?' Peggy could feel her blood boiling. 'What about me?'

'You? You're still only a child, Peggy. Someone has to be in charge … to take care of you just like a mother …'

'A mother! A mother!' Hot tears pricked Peggy's eyes. 'You! You're not my mother!'

Eily's face went pale. In that instant Peggy felt the sting of a slap across her face.

'I hate you!' screamed Peggy. 'I hate you! I hate you …' She kept shouting it as she pushed open the back door and ran down the narrow alley that led to Market Lane.

Two women were gossiping on a doorstep and stopped in mid-conversation to stare at her. She stuck out her tongue at them and ran hell-for-leather through the back end of Castletaggart towards the old bridge and river. She hoped there would be no one there.

Her prayers were answered. The place was deserted.

She leant over the low stone bridge. Beneath it the water flowed strongly, dragging the riverweed forwards. She stared into the river, blocking out the town from her sight and her mind.

Anger and disappointment raged inside her.

I won't forget about going. She can't treat me like a baby! she thought.

Her breath came in gulps and tore her throat.

It's not fair!

She was almost hypnotised by the movement of the sparkling water below and fascinated as her tears plopped into it and disappeared. Absentmindedly she put her hand up to rub her eyes. Her cheekbones smarted. She shook her head and watched the fine dust of white flour speckle the water. A tiny silver fish darted out from beneath a rock, opened its round mouth and swallowed bit after bit of it. Peggy began to giggle and shook her fingers over the water, watching the fish gobble each speck.

Already she felt calmer. In the distance she could hear a cuckoo. A forest of oaks and beech trees ran along the far side of the river, the fast-flowing water providing protection for the birds and animals against the people of the town.

This was a special place, a place where town and country met. It was her favourite spot in the whole of Castletaggart. Very few people bothered with this bridge. It was usually quiet down here, whilst the main town bridge always seemed to have crowds of people hanging around it.

Peggy pulled herself up on the bridge wall and sat on the uneven stone. She let her bare feet dangle over the clear sparkling water below.

Sometimes she'd sit here for hours, it was always so peaceful. Ever since she was a little girl it was the place she ran to ...

She remembered running away down here the very first morning she was meant to go to her new school in Castletaggart. But her two old great-aunts found her just as she was about to throw her new shoes into the river. They loved Peggy and her brother and sister so much. Auntie Nano had begun to give out to her, but Auntie Lena had coaxed and cajoled her away from the bridge and helped put the black sturdy laced shoes back on. Peggy smiled to herself. Even at seven years of age she'd been a little devil. Auntie Lena had understood her worries about starting school. All the other children had Mammies to take them there.

They had marched her back to the door of the bakery shop, and then with Eily coming along too, they had all set off together through Castletaggart to school. It was early morning on a glorious autumn day, all the shops were starting to open up and droves of children were headed in the same direction towards the small white-washed building which shone like a beacon at the top of Castletaggart Hill. At the school gate a fit of shyness and pure fear shook Peggy.

The two old ladies hugged her, then Eily squeezed her hand and walked her right up to the green wooden door. Just as she was about to run into the large school-room to try and get a seat on the bench beside her friend Julia, she looked back.

Nano and Lena stood ramrod stiff and straight and proud in the middle of the group of mothers anxiously waiting at the gate. And even from a distance Peggy could see that Eily's blue eyes were filled with tears – as if she was one of the mothers …

'Peggy! Peggy!' The call jolted her out of her dream.

She looked up. A wave of guilt washed over her. Eily was standing a few yards away, wiping her hands on her apron.

'I knew I'd find you here. I'm so sorry, Peggy!'

'Oh, Eily, I shouldn't have said what I said!'

'Still, I shouldn't have slapped you.'

'I really am sorry – 'twas a dreadful thing to say.' Peggy jumped down and ran and hugged her older sister. 'Let's go home,' she said.

They walked slowly back towards the shop. They passed a row of old cottages, every single one of them empty. Those occupants who hadn't died during the Great Famine had long since abandoned them and left Castletaggart.

'God, this place is getting fierce shabby,' muttered Eily. 'At this rate there won't be a sinner left here soon.'

Peggy bit her lip and fought the impulse to say I told you so.

'Look, Peggy! Kennys' drapery store has closed down.' Eily stopped and peered in through the planks that boarded up the vacant shop window. 'Not a thing in the place!'

Peggy stood on tiptoe so that she could see in. Every shelf was empty and a roll of dusty material lay forlornly on the counter. It seemed that every day a little bit more of Castletaggart changed. The town was no longer the busy place Peggy and Michael and Eily had finally arrived at, starving and homeless, nearly seven years ago in the middle of the Great Famine.

'Come on, Peggy! We'd better get a move on or all my baking will be up in smoke,' joked Eily. 'Anyways, I don't like leaving Nano on her own.'

The two of them quickened their pace until they reached the small shabby bakery shop at the bottom of Market Lane that was home.

'Run up and say hello to Nano, Peggy, but mind you don't say a word about the notice – there's no need to upset her!'

CHAPTER 2

Changes

THAT EVENING THE FOUR OF them sat around the table in the small cosy kitchen.

'You're the best cook in the world, Eily,' declared Michael, helping himself to some more stew. Peggy noticed that Eily barely touched her own food. It was so frustrating for her, baking and cooking, and then at the end of the day having so little to show for her hard work.

But customers were thin on the ground. A boy from the butcher's in the Main Street had left in a sheet of figures – another overdue account. And the flour barrel was only a third full.

'I'm working at the Big House tomorrow afternoon and evening, Peggy, so you'll have to give Nano a hand with the shop,' said Eily. Peggy nodded. 'No running off or forgetting about it!'

'Is there no chance of a job for you there?' asked Michael.

'If there was any kind of kitchen job going it would be mine. But you know yourself it's hard enough for them to keep the staff they have already.'

'Well, let's be grateful for the few hours of work you

do get there when they're extra busy,' urged Nano.

'Oh, I'm going daft. I nearly forgot to tell you, Nano, I met the landlord up at the cattle market. He said he'd drop into the shop within the next day or two,' said Michael.

'Billy Kelly! What would he want?' Nano was worried. 'Is it about the rent do you think?'

Peggy was just dying to talk about the notice on the dresser.

'Not tonight,' mouthed Eily.

Michael disappeared off to help a friend with milking and Nano got up from the table and wandered into the empty shop. 'It's the only place I can find time to think.'

Eily ran upstairs to change. Peggy whistled as she cleared up and brushed the floor. Hearing a tap on the small window, she stopped and ran to the door.

'Good evening, Peggy!'

'Come on in, John, she'll be down in a minute.'

The young farmer stepped in and sat down near the range to wait for Eily. Out of the corner of her eye, Peggy studied him. He was tall and kind of handsome with thick black curls. His hands and face were tanned and weather-beaten from working out in the fields, and although his clothes were clean, his jacket needed patching and his shirt was frayed. He was very quiet, but Eily seemed to be mad about him. Young love – that's what Nano always whispered when she saw them together.

Eily smiled and put on her shawl when she saw John Powers.

'We're going up the town for a bit of a walk. Will you finish up here, Peggy? And don't forget to warm some milk later to help Nano sleep.'

'I'll be fine,' said Peggy smirking, watching them walk arm in arm down the lane. Eily deserved some happiness.

Later Peggy tiptoed into the darkened shop. It was small and clean. On one wall the shelves were stacked with jars of preserves – chutneys and jellies and jams; the other counter was for the daily bake – soda bread, brown bread, wheaten loaf, scones and fancy breads. The smell of the hot bread would fill the shop and the street. There was a small drawer unit which held fancy bakery items like glacé cherries, sugared violets, marzipan fruits.

Nano was sitting in her old chair rocking backwards and forwards. She always did that when she was worried or troubled.

* * *

The next afternoon the shop bell rang. Peggy looked through the kitchen door and saw Eily talking to Billy Kelly, the landlord. She motioned to Peggy to get Nano.

'Auntie Nano, come quick, Mr Kelly's in the shop. He wants to talk to you.'

'Fetch me my good shawl – yes, the black one, pet, – and will you tidy my hair a bit at the back there please.'

Peggy got the bristle brush, re-did the bun of hair and fixed it tight with a few extra hairpins. Nano was anxious, but managed to appear serene as she walked into the shop, shook Mr Kelly by the hand and sat down in her chair.

'Girls, will one of ye fetch this good man a cup of tea, and how about a slice of that fresh apple and cinnamon tart you made this morning, Eily?'

'That would be grand, Miss Murphy, thank you,' replied Mr Kelly.

He was a tall, thin, nervous type of man and he paced around the room a few times, before finally sitting down.

'I don't exactly know where to start,' he mumbled.

'The beginning – 'tis usually the best place,' smiled Nano, sensing his nervousness.

'Well, Miss Murphy, I've come along today to ask you if you'd be interested in buying this piece of property outright. You've been a tenant for nigh on forty years.'

Nano let out her breath with a gasp. 'Oh, Mr Kelly, you must know that if I had enough savings I'd have bought the shop long ago.'

'Miss Murphy, the asking price would not be too high. I know myself the roof is sagging and in need of repair,' he pleaded. 'Isn't there any way you could afford it?'

Nano didn't say a word, but just shook her head slowly from side to side. Peggy passed her a cup of weak tea. She sipped it and stared at the man beside her.

'Mr Kelly, will I tell you something?' she said at last. 'You are the living image of your late father, Tom. He was a good man too ...'

'My father was fond of you and your sister and we always had the finest cakes in the town on rent day.' He tried to smile. 'Miss Murphy, you can see yourself how bad things are in the town. I'm a married man myself with four young children, but even with five pieces of property, things are not good. People can't afford to pay their rent.'

Nano began to apologise. 'Are we late with our rent again?'

'No, listen, Miss Murphy, that's not what I'm here about. The truth is I am selling off all my interests in the town and moving to Dublin with my family. I have a brother who has his own business there.' He stopped. 'What will become of us? Are we going to lose the roof over our heads? What about the three children?'

'I'm sorry, there's nothing more I can do. I need to raise funds myself. The O'Donnells and the Kennys have accepted assisted passage to America. I'm not the only landlord forced to do this. A group of us are trying our best to look after our tenants, so letters of application for a ship's voucher have been delivered to many in this part of the town.'

Eily and Peggy stared at Nano. Her face was as pale as snow and her lips looked blue.

'It came yesterday,' Peggy said and ran to the kitchen dresser to get it.

Nano stared at it blankly. 'So you want to pack me off on one of those old coffin ships to the New World, is that it?'

'No, Miss Murphy. It's just that many people want to go to America. We're only offering to help them. The youngsters might consider it,' he finished off lamely.

'How long have I got left here?' Nano asked.

'It will take a bit of time to find a buyer, though there is someone interested. I suppose a few weeks.'

Nano stood up. 'I'm not blaming you, Mr Kelly, and I'm only glad that my poor sister Lena never lived to see this day. Thank you for coming to see me.'

Peggy watched as the landlord bade his embarrassed goodbyes.

'Are you all right, Nano?' asked Eily.

The old lady stood up. 'I'm away to my bed, we'll talk about this later.' She muttered under her breath, obviously exhausted from the strain.

Peggy and Eily looked at each other. They both knew that closing the shop was enough to break their great-aunt's heart.

* * *

It was almost midnight. Eily, Michael and Peggy sat by the range, arguing back and forth about their future.

'Why can't we all go to America?' questioned Peggy. 'That's the simplest thing to do. Our passage will be paid.'

'That's no answer, Peggy!' said Eily sternly. 'Do you think poor Nano would survive such a voyage?'

Peggy, defeated, shook her head and added a whispered 'No.'

'Auntie Nano and Auntie Lena took us in when we had no one or no home. You remember, both of you, the state the three of us were in when we arrived here after weeks on the road and how the two of them cared for us and got us well again? They could have put us in a workhouse or orphans' home, but instead we became their family. They fed us even though food was scarce and they brought us up. Never, never would I leave poor Nano – she's all on her own now. It's our turn to look after her.' Eily's cheeks blazed.

'Maybe if I went I'd get a job fairly easy and be able to

send some money home for the rest of you,' suggested Michael.

'I could work too,' added Peggy. 'I'm all but finished school, and you know well there are no jobs here. They say there's plenty of jobs across the ocean.' Eily started to shake her head. 'No, no, I don't want you to go. The three of us have been together always. We can't split up now. Peggy's only a baby. Who'd look after her?'

'I'm not a baby. I'm thirteen and old enough to be in service,' cried Peggy indignantly.

'Look, Eily, if you're going to stay and look after Nano you'll need money,' said Michael.

'If there were jobs here we'd get them, but there aren't any. So what else can we do?' asked Peggy.

'Eily, you know Peggy's right. The two of us could go to America. I'm getting fed up hanging around here day in, day out, helping at the market sometimes or with milking or odd farm jobs. I want a proper job. Eily, I'll fill in the application anyway for Peggy and myself, it won't do any harm.'

'The Molloys are going and the O'Caseys, so we wouldn't be on our own …' Peggy began.

'I need time to think about it. We all have to try and work out what's the best thing to do. Come on away to bed or we'll be exhausted in the morning. Let's all say a prayer that something will be sorted out,' said Eily.

* * *

Two days later Eily told Michael there might be a vacancy for him up at Castletaggart House. A wide grin spread across his face. Maybe he could get a job at last.

Eily had been helping in the kitchens at a ball in the Big House the night before. As usual, she asked the cook if there were any vacancies. The woman shook her head.

'Not unless you want to help with the horses in the stables?' she joked. 'The stable boy has just left after getting a bad kick from a mare and the head groom wants someone good and gentle with animals and unafraid of horses.'

Eily straight away mentioned her brother and his way with animals and love of horses.

Michael couldn't believe it. Horses – working with them, grooming them, feeding them, cleaning them and maybe riding them. It would be a miracle if he could get it.

'Stable boy, stable boy,' no matter how often he said it, it sounded good. 'Are you sure, Eily?'

His older sister nodded. 'I'm not codding you, Michael. Honest to God, it's a great opportunity.'

'Eily, I'll do my best to get that job. It's all I ever wanted.'

Peggy smiled. Michael was so lucky. But what would happen to their plans if he got the job? she wondered.

Nano blessed herself. 'Thanks be to God,' she murmured, but added, 'We mustn't count our chickens before they're hatched.' Peggy loved her aunt and her old sayings.

Eily seemed embarrassed. She poured out another cup of tea.

'Well, I've a bit more news.' She looked up. 'John has asked me to marry him.'

Three pairs of eyes fixed on Eily's glowing face.

'You said yes, Eily! Oh you did say yes,' urged Peggy,

squeezing her sister's hand. Eily shyly tossed back her long fair hair. 'Well, I suppose, sort of … there are lots of things to be considered.' However it was clear to them all that Eily was brimming over with happiness.

'How are John and his father managing up on the farm?' asked Nano. 'I hope poor old Josh hasn't had one of his turns recently?'

Everyone in Castletaggart knew about Joshua Powers. At the height of the Great Famine he had lost his wife, two sons and young daughter to famine fever. Joshua roamed his fields, flinging sods of turf and stones at the sky and cursing God for what he had done. He spent five days like that until John, his eldest son, got him calmed down. However, from time to time the memory would come back and he would rant and rave and curse and wander the fields again. Locally he was known as Cursing Josh Powers.

Nano looked at Eily, Michael and Peggy and thanked the heavens that God had sent these special children to herself and Lena. Large tears filled her eyes and she took out her big white hanky and blew her nose loudly.

Eily looked over at her. 'Auntie Nano, don't tell me you're crying with happiness? Aren't you the silly one!' Eily put her arms around the old lady, sensing her sadness. 'Don't fret. Powers' cottage may be a bit small, but there'll be space for you. You don't think I'd run off and leave you on your own? Nano, there's a little room that used to be John's sister's – it'll be yours and Peggy'll have the settle bed in the kitchen.'

Peggy, who had been dreaming, suddenly snapped out of it. A settle bed up at Powers' farm, miles from the town and friends! No chance of a job, only helping Eily with the house! Peggy just managed to hold her tongue.

* * *

Peggy stood out in the yard. She dragged the soaking wet clothes from the bucket and started to stretch them across the rope that was strung across the cobbled yard.

Michael came out to join her.

'Are you going to give me a hand, Michael?' she joked.

Michael bent down and dragged out an old bed sheet. He let the water drip all over his shoes.

'Michael!' Peggy stared at him. 'What's wrong with you? Fling it up on the line before you soak yourself.'

'Peg, I want to talk to you.'

She looked at him. Something was up, she could tell.

'Spit it out, Michael, whatever it is.'

Michael blushed red as a turkey cock.

'I got the job, the one up at Castletaggart House.'

Peggy stared at her brother. She felt betrayed.

'I'll be living in over the stables. Imagine, they have twenty horses and I'll be helping to look after them all.'

'Oh, Michael,' Peggy swallowed hard, 'I'm so happy for you.'

'I never believed it would happen. All my life I've loved animals and wanted to work with them. You remember when I left school how hard I tried to get work on a farm. I thought it would never happen – and now!' Peggy pinned a smile across her face.

Michael stopped and looked right at her. 'Peggy, I suppose I'm letting you down. There's no need for me to go to America now. I never wanted to go anyway. I've got my chance here at home and I'll grab it.'

'I know, Michael. So now I'm on my own.'

'Don't be cross with me, Peggy. I'm real sorry, but this is my dream come true – working with horses. We all have dreams and must follow them, so Peggy, you must do what you want!' Michael lifted the empty enamel bucket. 'Eily and Nano think it's grand. In two days' time I'll be living in at the Big House.'

The next day a brown envelope was delivered, addressed to Michael and Margaret O'Driscoll. It contained another notice and two vouchers. The silver-printed vouchers could be used at Masters & McCabes Shipping Office at Queenstown 'as payment for passage to America. On receipt of said voucher a ticket would be issued to the bearer.' The notice gave details about emigration and advice on what to bring, and wished the applicants luck.

Michael glanced at his voucher, shrugged his shoulders and pushed it back in the envelope. He had other things on his mind.

Every hour or so, Peggy would take her voucher out and look at it. 'Passage to America' – the words burned in her mind.

'Eily, please, I could go on my own. I'd get a job straight away and I'd send money home,' Peggy pleaded.

'No! No! You're too young. You'd never survive in a strange country on your own,' Eily kept answering back.

'But I want to go. It's not just what you want, this is something *I* want!'

'At thirteen you think it's important what you want, you little devil!'

'At barely thirteen you saved Michael and me from the workhouse and brought us all the way from Duneen to Castletaggart. You pushed us and made us walk and got food for us and forced us to survive the Famine,' Peggy reminded her.

'That was different. I had no choice,' Eily admitted.

'But I feel I've no choice. The shop will close down. You and John will be getting married. I've seen Powers' cottage, there won't be space for me there. Nano is the one that needs a home. You've been trying to get work for the last two years and if you couldn't, how do you think I'd ever get a job?'

Peggy's question hung in the air.

Over the next few days she kept on asking and asking. She stuck out her chin and used every ounce of O'Driscoll stubbornness to get her way.

'Nano, if you were young, what would you do?' She forced her great-aunt to answer.

Nano rocked backwards and forwards and after much consideration grudgingly said: 'I'll tell you something, Peggy, if my sister Lena were still alive and the two of us were in our heyday and young, we would be the first ones to take a passage to America. Such a chance of an adventure we'd never have missed.'

She patted Peggy on the hand. 'I'll talk to Eily,' the old lady assured her.

That night there was a meeting in the back kitchen of Murphys' Bakery. Peggy stayed up in the bedroom as down below Nano, Eily and John Powers argued and discussed her future. She listened to the singsong of their voices, wondering what the outcome would be.

* * *

Eily's eyes were red-rimmed and her face was blotchy when she slowly climbed the stairs and came in to sit on Peggy's wooden bed.

'Well, Peggy!'

Peggy raised herself up in the bed. They hugged each other.

Eily looked tired. 'Yes. The answer is yes.' She tossed the envelope on to the beige blanket.

'Are you angry with me?' asked Peggy.

'No, pet, I'm not.' Eily sat down on the corner of the bed. 'I'm just sad. Sad for myself I suppose. I'll miss you. It'll be so lonely. Michael will be gone, and then if you're on the far side of the world …' she trailed off. 'Why do you have to go, Peggy? Don't you think you'd be happy with the rest of us on the farm?'

Peggy stared at the strands of wool in the blanket, and didn't answer.

Eily had begun to cry. 'It's just so sad. Oh, Peggy, you're my little sister. How can I ever let you go? I can't bear parting!'

'I know how you feel,' Peggy said. 'Do you remember the day that Mother left home to look for Father?' Eily looked puzzled but nodded. 'I wasn't even seven, but I can remember that awful day as if it was yesterday. I knew as she walked down that little road that she would never come back.'

'Peggy, none of us knew that. She was going to the roadworks to search for Father. We all thought she'd come back,' said Eily.

'No, I never believed it. I knew it would be the last

time I'd see her. We never saw her again. Sometimes I pretend it's that day again, just so I can remember her.'

'Oh, Peggy, you poor little pet, we all miss her and Father. Day in, day out, for the first two years, every time that shop bell downstairs rang I'd run into the shop just in case one of them would be standing there looking for us.'

'I did the same,' whispered Peggy. 'Sometimes I'm scared, Eily, that I won't remember them. I even try to think what Mother looked like to remind myself.'

Eily got up from the bed, picked up an oval-shaped mirror and held it in front of Peggy's face.

'Look, Peggy, look at yourself. You look just like her.'

Peggy stared at the round face under a mop of thick chestnut-coloured hair, the two big brown eyes and neat slightly tilted nose, the freckles and small white teeth.

'When you go away, Peggy, what will I have to remind me of you and Mother?' sighed Eily.

Peggy hugged her. 'You're the most important person in the world to me, Eily. You've loved me like a mother, yet you're my sister and my best friend. Nothing will change that,' she whispered.

'Peggy, I can't understand you – aren't you frightened about going? About the ship, and America, and being on your own?' asked Eily.

'No, no. I remember things that were worse, a lot worse,' said Peggy firmly.

'I'll talk to the schoolmaster tomorrow,' said Eily. 'And do you know Nell Molloy? I heard herself and her family are going to America too. I'll call up and talk to her, she might keep an eye on you. And I suppose we'd better bake a mountain of oatcakes as they're meant to be the best thing to last the long journey.'

CHAPTER 3

Farewell

AT SUNDAY MASS FATHER LYNCH called out the list of names of those who were emigrating and recited a special prayer for them. Peggy fixed her gaze on the carved wooden cross as she felt the eyes of the congregation stare at her when her name was called out. Afterwards many people came to shake her hand and wish her luck. Eily and Nano stood on either side of her like two statues.

That evening Market Lane was crowded as the neighbours came and went to say their goodbyes. Michael had managed to get a few hours off. The small kitchen was packed and Nano and Eily had laid on a bit of a spread – soda bread, scones and two huge porter cakes. Plates and cups sparkled in the firelight. Two jars of poteen stood on the dresser and a barrel of porter was dripping a cream of froth onto the red tiled floor.

It was a wake of sorts – a farewell party, and everyone knew that it was unlikely they would ever set eyes again on Peggy O'Driscoll in this lifetime.

John Joe Daly's arrival was greeted with a cheer. He pulled out his fiddle with a flourish and began to play a few notes to warm up.

Peggy looked at all the friends and neighbours. Hard lives and bad times and yet they could still smile. I'll never meet the likes again, she said to herself, sealing their faces and stories into her memory. John Joe was now ready and began to send his music tripping across the room. Two little girls from Market Square who went to Peggy's school got up and began to dance, hopping like two fairy children, their backs straight and their hair bouncing in the air, their narrow pointed feet flying as if they had a life of their own. Their father leant against the door smoking his clay pipe and bursting with pride when loud clapping rewarded their performance.

Michael, blushing, stood in front of Nano and bowed extravagantly. The old lady got up from the rocking chair and took the floor. John Joe slowed the music so that the audience could appreciate Nano's intricate steps. Michael guided her gently round the room. Peggy stared at him. He was so handsome. All his gentleness and care seemed to make him stronger. Her brother was turning into a fine young man. Peggy bit her lip. Pin-pricks of tears were trying to push behind her eyes – she must deny them. Nano caught her eye and ended her dance with a fine display of petticoat and then collapsed in Michael's arms laughing out loud.

A few minutes later half the room was up, joining in a lively reel. Peggy was spun from one strong pair of arms to another till she was so out of breath she couldn't even talk. Kate Connolly got up and sang two songs. The time seemed to fly. Peggy knew everyone was talking about her – in some ways it was if she had already gone.

Eventually all the well-wishers left and it was just themselves again. Michael made a cup of tea for Nano. She looked exhausted. 'Never did I think, nearly seven years ago when Lena and I found three raggy little ones standing in our kitchen, of the happiness and love you'd bring into our old lives. And now the fledglings are leaving the nest. I can't help myself feeling sad no matter how proud of the three of ye I am,' she said.

Peggy looked at her. The soft grey-blue eyes were misty.

'Come on, Auntie Nano, away to bed, you're all done in. A good night's sleep will have you right as rain in the morning. Away up and I'll sit with you till you drop off.'

Peggy grabbed her aunt's shawl and followed her up the stairs, a sudden stab of thought making her realise that this was the last time. Nano changed into her nightdress and let Peggy brush her hair. She was just about to get into bed when she went over to the old oak chest of drawers. From the bottom drawer she drew out a big leather-covered book.

'Sit down, Peggy, till I give you this.'

The girl looked at the familiar cover with its design of harps and leaves.

'Do you remember? This was Lena's Bible and now I'm passing it on to you.'

Peggy opened the cover. Lena Murphy was written on the inside in big bold letters. Further on, two blank pages had been covered with names and birth dates. It was the family tree. Peggy ran her fingers across the line with her mother's date of birth – 5 November 1814 – and the date of her marriage to John O'Driscoll. Auntie Lena had written underneath: Died during Ireland's Great Famine, and she had also written: Mary Ellen (Eily), Michael and Margaret (Peggy), Baby Bridget (in Heaven), and their dates of birth.

Two pairs of eyes met and Peggy realised that it was more than just a Bible she was being handed. It was her history – the keeping of a tradition. No more words were needed. She hugged Nano and ran from the room. The lump in her throat was so big it nearly choked her.

Peggy crawled into her own bedroom. She felt as if every bit of adventure and spirit had oozed out of her. The night was suddenly chilly and she pulled the blanket up over her. A few minutes later Eily came in. She looked bone-tired and weary. She pulled on her nightgown and climbed in beside Peggy.

'You're not asleep, Peggy, are you?'

Peggy shook her head and reached for her sister's shoulder.

'Don't cry, little sister,' urged Eily, though large tears like crystals were streaming down her own face. Peggy hiccupped and then began to giggle. Eily started to tickle her. She knew all the best places. The two of them were in stitches when Michael stuck his head in.

'Shush! You'll wake Nano up!' Michael came and sat on the end of the bed. The three of them together. It had been like this for so long. They talked and talked, about the years behind and the years ahead. Nothing would break that bond. The birds had just started their dawn chorus when Eily insisted they must all have some rest.

* * *

No matter what she did, Peggy couldn't sleep. She was too excited, too nervous, too sad – too everything. Gently she rolled over on her side and eased herself out of the bed. Eily slept on.

Peggy pulled on some clothes and crept like a kitten from the room and down the stairs to the kitchen. She lifted the latch and let herself out.

There wasn't a sinner around. Everyone was still in bed. Peggy was tempted to shout: Today's the day! Wake up! but she held her peace and escaped from the narrow streets and alleyways. She passed the little bridge and this morning it seemed lonelier than ever. But she didn't have time to sit and dream today. Small-holdings where potatoes would soon be ready, rich meadows of lush green grass and fields of grain – barley and wheat – spread out in the distance.

She climbed over a jagged low wall into her favourite field. The grass was damp with dew, making her feet wet and the hem of her dress cling to her legs. Cowslips and buttercups, bluebells, ragged robin, tall lacy cow parsley – all slept drowsily waiting for the morning sun to wake them up. She picked them one by one, and pulled ribbons of woodbine from the hedgerow. She danced and spun round and round till the blue sky and green grass blurred and became one. Her arms were filled with wild flowers when she suddenly noticed an old farmer and his cart slow down and stare at her, curious. Soon the town would be awake. She raced back to Market Lane and pushed in the kitchen door.

Nano was sitting at the kitchen table in her night-dress. She looked old and tired, and beautiful.

Peggy ran to her. 'Aren't they lovely, Nano?' She

opened her arms and let the flowers tumble onto her great-aunt's lap. 'They're for you.'

'Peggy, you're always bringing me flowers ...' Nano held the woodbine to her face. 'By tonight its scent will fill the house ... by tonight ...'

Peggy washed and dressed. Eily cooked the biggest breakfast ever. They all sat around and watched her eat, making sure she swallowed every bit. Eily had sorted out food for travelling, saying she hoped it would last all the weeks at sea. There was dried beef, some tea and sugar, a rich porter cake, a round golden cheese, and dry oatcakes. Another hour and it would be time to leave.

Nano was varying between fussing and flustering and sitting down every few minutes with her handkerchief to her eyes. Peggy tried to leave her be and concentrate on getting ready.

Michael fastened a horse-hair bracelet on Peggy's wrist. 'From the three best horses in the stable.' He had plaited and linked the black, the chestnut brown and the golden hair so they came together and formed a stiff circle. 'It will bring you luck and speed and strength,' he added.

Peggy looked at it and loved it straight away, knowing what it meant.

Nano produced a small drawstring purse, heavy with coins. 'For a rainy day, pet, and to help you get started.'

Eily wrapped her best shawl around Peggy's shoulders. 'It's yours. We can't send you off to the New World with a worn-out shawl.' Peggy clutched it close to her. She rubbed her face to the soft wool. It would enfold her just like Eily had always wrapped her and kept her safe.

All too soon they heard the clatter of the cart on the

cobbles in the lane. Nell Molloy and her family were sitting on the cart, the little ones perched on tightly wrapped bundles of clothes. Michael went to fetch Peggy's bundle. Eily was stacking her wrapped food.

Nano had disappeared into the shop. She was walking up and down and running her hand over and back on the counter distractedly. Peggy tiptoed in and hugged her.

'Stay here, Auntie Nano! Don't come out in the lane.'

Nano managed to paste a wobbly smile across her face. There'd be time enough for tears later.

Michael lifted Peggy on to the cart. Eily ran almost the whole way down the main street, waving, and following the cart and horses like a little girl. Peggy watched and waved until all that was left of Castletaggart town was the haze of smoke disappearing in the distance.

CHAPTER 4

Queenstown

 THE CART JUMPED AND JOLTED along the bumpy roads and tracks, the two horses trotting in time, their manes blowing in the breeze. Nell Molloy was busy keeping order among her brood, who were singing and playing tricks. After a few miles they would pick up the Sullivan brothers.

This is travelling in style, thought Peggy as she let her feet hang over the side, free and easy. Father Lynch had paid for the cart. He regularly told a story of a husband and wife and child who had been on their last legs at the height of the Famine. The good father gave them a meal and paid their passage for America, but a week later he discovered that they had died on the way to the harbour, too weak and worn out to make the journey to the sea port. Ever since, Father Lynch pledged that anyone from Castletaggart parish who was setting sail for the New World would have the comfort of a good ride on the first step of their journey. No one would leave the town in shame or despondent if Father Lynch had any say in it. There had been too much of that.

The summer countryside flew by. Mile after mile blended into a confusion of colour and images – green hedgerows, wild honeysuckle, high, heavy hawthorns weighed down with boughs full of blossom, small woods of ancient oak and ash where startled wood pigeons broke out in a flap into the clear blue sky.

'I told your aunt and your sister I'd keep a good eye on you,' announced Mrs Molloy. She was a big woman and was already hot and sweaty with the heat and all the excitement. 'Though I know what a good wee lass you are. We'll all look out for each other.'

'Thanks,' mumbled Peggy, grabbing the youngest boy before he fell off the cart.

His mother whacked him on the bottom and told him to 'sit down proper' or there'd be no ship for him. Peggy took out some homemade toffee and shared it among the children. Tess Donlon's toffee was guaranteed to keep anybody busy for a while.

Nell shook her head when it was offered. 'No, pet, keep it for yourself.' Over the next half-hour she told Peggy about her husband, Dan, who had gone to America two years before and had worked like a horse to save enough to send some money home and put more aside towards a place of their own in America. The family were getting assistance towards their passage and, God willing, would forget the horrors of the past and start a new life once they reached foreign shores.

The two Sullivan boys climbed on at Mulligs' Cross. Peggy had never seem them look so neat and tidy. Their hair was washed and cut and their faces shone and looked well scrubbed. Their clothes were worn but clean. There was no trace of the usual grime and dirt that clung to them when they hung around Market Square in Castletaggart. The younger, Liam, who was about fifteen, whistled out loud. The very air rang with laughter and noise as they trundled on.

They passed villages and farms and small towns. When they came to an incline most of them would get off and old Francie would coax the horses upwards, patting their necks and talking softly to them. They stopped from time to time to rest the animals. After about five hours they were all exhausted, but at last they felt a tang in the air.

'The sea breeze,' announced Nell Molloy. Everyone perked up. 'Breathe in that good salt air, 'tis great for the lungs,' she urged.

They had turned off a busy road, crossed a narrow bridge at the estuary of a river where they saw a small stone tower, and now began a fairly steep ascent. They all got off the cart except Nell and the youngest child.

Through thick shrubs and hedges Peggy caught fleeting glimpses of blue. Suddenly they turned a corner and found they were right in Queenstown. The town was built on a steep hill which towered over the vast blueness of the sea below. Huge seabirds flapped lazily in the clear sky, their sounds filling the air.

Peggy had never seen anything like it before. Busy shops and stalls crowded the front where people pushed and shoved to spend their money. There was a holiday atmosphere. The water lapped against the shore wall and bobbed and shone in the sunshine. Across from Queenstown were two islands, and outside lay the open sea. Crowds of ships jostled for space in the harbour; there were fishing boats and three- and four-masted packet ships. A large ship disappeared over the horizon.

They all lifted their things off the cart and placed

them on the ground, unsure what to do next.

'I must be getting back to Castletaggart after I water the horses and rest them a while,' said Francie. 'The best thing is to get yourselves to the shipping office up the street.' He pointed. 'Best of luck to each and every one of ye,' he added, shaking each one by the hand, right down to little Tim. They watched as their last link with Castletaggart vanished down a cobbled laneway.

Mrs Molloy led the way and they all trooped over to the large stone building with the painted wooden façade, with Masters & McCabes Shipping inscribed on it in gold letters. Against the outside wall a wooden board carried a poster with details of the different vessels and their destinations, ships to Liverpool and New York.

Young Tim and Nellie stayed outside while the rest of them went in to see what was what. There was a long wooden bench on one side of the room and they all took a seat. A few minutes later a clerk beckoned to Nell. She stood against the counter, chatting with him.

Next it was Peggy's turn. She took out the notice and voucher from a hidden pocket sewn inside her skirt. The man looked tired and old. He studied Peggy and examined both pieces of paper.

Peggy looked at her hands and tried not to appear nervous. After a nod of his head he disappeared into a back room and came back with a brown ledger. He opened it and wrote down the date and Peggy's name and address.

'Age?' he queried.

'Just fourteen.'

'Are you or are you not fourteen?' he insisted.

'I will be … in a few days,' stuttered Peggy, trying to

make herself look taller and older – and lying.

She could feel herself blushing, and her right leg was beginning to hop – it always began to shake when she was nervous. What in heaven's name would she do if he wouldn't let her travel?

'Humph … well … occupation?'

'Domestic,' said Peggy firmly, pulling her shawl tighter around her and looking him square in the eye. He closed the ledger and then went over to the clerk that Nell was with and pulled the black and red book over to his part of the counter.

Written on top of the page were the words: Passenger List. He scrawled in Peggy's name and details. Then he opened a drawer and from the top of a pile took a big beige ticket with black writing on it and a drawing of part of a ship.

'You will travel on *The Fortunata*, which will leave here in two days' time and is bound for Boston. You will travel steerage, and meals and fresh water will be provided. Have you a member of family or someone to assist you on arrival?'

Peggy stood open-mouthed, wondering what answer she should give.

Nell came over, her own business complete. 'My own darling husband is there, setting up things for us the past two years, and this is my poor dead sister's child. Sure we couldn't leave her behind and us all going to a new life.'

The man nodded and scribbled in the book again.

Once outside the door Peggy hugged Nell. 'I owe you, thanks!' she said as she whistled for joy, the ticket in her hand.

'Now, missee, quiet down,' urged Nell. 'We have to find a place to stay until our ship sails. Up the hill there's a place with large rooms and plenty of beds I'm told.'

They trudged up the hill and found a shabby house with a wooden sign over the door saying: Lodgings – Sea View. Peggy and Nell went in. Nell did all the talking and the surly middle-aged woman finally sighed and told them to bring in the children. They ignored the filthy stairs and the smell of cabbage that permeated the whole house, and followed the woman upstairs. The Sullivan boys and young Tom and Tim took the smaller room and the girls and Nell had the other.

Peggy looked around. There was a small window, so dirty you could hardly see through it, a large double bed and a smaller one put up in the corner. The blankets looked faded and worn and the bed itself creaked and squeaked when little Nellie and Mary sat on it. They stored their stuff for travelling neatly in the corner of the room.

'We need a good meal to set us up,' said Nell. 'I'll ask the lady of the house about it.'

An hour later they sat around the large kitchen table in the damp, steamy kitchen. A thin slice of greyish bacon and a mound of potatoes and cabbage were served to all. Their landlady also grudgingly agreed to provide porridge in the morning for a small extra contribution. The chat and tricks of the little ones soon made everyone forget about the over-cooked meal and they agreed to stretch their legs and have a proper look around the town afterwards.

Once darkness fell, Nell felt the family should be in

bed. They returned to Sea View. Despite its drabness and discomfort, exhaustion and excitement got the better of them and in no time they were all fast asleep.

CHAPTER 5

The Fortunata

PEGGY WOKE FIRST. LITTLE TIM had abandoned the boys' room next door and lay sprawled beside his mother. The two little girls were curled up together near the edge of the bed. All were still in a deep sleep.

Peggy tiptoed over to the window and peered through the faded floral curtains. It was early morning and the small fishing boats could be spotted in the distance, treading out to the open sea to search for their day's catch – and then she noticed it! Through the gaps of the houses, there, clear as day, a large sailing ship, its soaring masts reaching to the sky, higher than all the others.

'*The Fortunata*,' she whispered to herself, 'it's here.' She was tempted to shout it out loud and wake the others up, but she resisted.

She crept back to bed, pulled the blanket up around her and fell into a strange dreamy sleep: she was dressed in a beautiful white dress and Eily was calling her and yet she was dancing and spinning and wouldn't stop to answer her.

'Peggy! Peggy! The ship is here!' Little Tim was clambering all over her and shaking her head with his sticky little hands.

Nell and the girls were standing at the window, bursting with excitement and wiping the sleepy-heads out of their eyes. Peggy yawned and hopped out of bed.

'Look, Peggy,' said Mary, 'do you see it? Isn't it grand. Our ship is in.'

Getting a family dressed and fed was never accomplished in such a short time. The six of them raced down the steep hill of Queenstown to the quayside. A thrill of excitement ran through Peggy when she saw *The Fortunata*.

'It's huge,' gasped Tim.

Giant masts towered above the ship, and a maze of ropes and pulleys criss-crossed backwards and forwards. A cabin boy swung from a rope ladder high above their heads, his tricks earning gasps of admiration from the people below. The sails were rolled up tightly. Two young seamen sat cross-legged on the deck, repairing a wide piece of white canvas. The wooden deck was polished and shone but the under-side of the ship was covered with grey barnacles and slimy green seaweed.

Sailors were busy unloading large bales of cotton, some chests of tea, and a quantity of timber, all being stacked in piles along the quay. They shouted gruffly at the children to 'Get away out of it and don't damage those goods.' The quay was packed with people trying to get a look at *The Fortunata*, all fellow passengers no doubt.

The next day was the longest ever. Everything was packed and ready to go except the ship. Provisions were being loaded on board and Nell kept fussing over whether she had brought enough with her to keep them going. On the whispered advice of the landlady she had decided to invest in a chamber pot and a tin bucket.

'You'll thank me, Mrs, mark my words,' assured the landlady, pointing Nell in the direction of a hardware shop down the lane which had the best bargains. Peggy had grudgingly taken out some of her money and chipped in towards the cost and was now a part owner of them.

By four o'clock a queue had formed on the quayside. Peggy stood in line, just behind Nell and holding little Nellie by the hand. The children were whingeing and whining and no one could blame them as it was nearly six o'clock by the time they reached the top of the queue. Their names were called out and checked off the ship's list. They walked across a narrow gangplank which opened straight into the steerage area underneath the deck.

It was just terrible. Not what they expected at all. They stepped down into a wide dark gloomy area where small, narrow bunks were crowded together. No one would fit in them surely, thought Peggy. They had raised wooden edges along the sides. Everybody was pushing and shoving, trying to get into steerage. It was cramped already beyond imagination and yet more and more passengers kept filing down.

'Grab some bunks, Mary, quick, make a run for it.' Dragging the children with her, Nell gathered up their baggage and flung the whole lot towards two bunks, one on top of the other. She shoved the bucket and pot under the lower one. Another woman was trying to put a blanket on the top bunk.

'Mrs, my children are sitting in that bunk, have you no eyes in your head?' yelled Nell.

'There's no windows, Mammy,' wailed Mary.

'No single bunks,' shouted a ginger-haired sailor. 'Two or three to a bunk. We're heavily booked so everyone shares.'

Peggy stood rooted to the spot. She felt so alone she just didn't know what to do. Suddenly Nell ran over, grabbed Peggy's bundle and threw it on the top bunk with the girls' things.

'Peggy, aren't you in a right daze. Sure, you'll be sleeping with Nellie and Mary. I'll be below with the boys. We'll stick together through all this.'

Silent, Peggy climbed up on top. She sat on the worn wooden slats and watched the chaos all around her. As every family came aboard the mad scramble for a place became desperate. Single people, widows and orphans stood in the centre of the steerage area, unsure what they should do. In the end, a sailor allotted them a space to share. It was humiliating. God knows how it would be having to share such closeness with total strangers, thought Peggy.

Down below, Nell had relaxed and was chatting to the woman in the bunk beside her. 'The minute I saw this place I was determined it would be ours. Look, Mrs, there's a little hatch there to let some air in and the table is near enough without being too close, if you get my meaning, and isn't there the extra bonus of a nice neighbour like yourself thrown in.

'I'm Nell Molloy and this is my brood – Mary, young Nellie, Thomas and Tim – and not forgetting Peggy O'Driscoll, as near family as you can get.'

Peggy smiled but was too busy watching all that was going on to want to get involved in stories and family histories. Along the centre of the lower deck were fixed sturdy oak tables with a long bench on either side. This was their dining area; obviously they would take turns using the tables.

Within an hour and a half, calm had descended on *The Fortunata*.

It was dim and gloomy down below. Peggy couldn't believe that this dreadful place was where she would spend the next five to six weeks. She could see so much in the faces of fellow passengers – excitement, hope, fear and, in a few, utter misery. They all were aware of the noise of water slapping against the wood of the ship's frame. Suddenly it seemed louder and stronger, and they realised that the ship was casting off and leaving the quayside.

'We're away, she's sailing,' someone shouted.

At once there was a mad rush up on deck. They formed a human chain all round the ship. No words were spoken as they feasted their eyes on a last look at Ireland. The sailors raced around, some away up above the deck balancing on the tall masts, others dragging on the thick curving ropes as the heavy canvas sails began to catch the wind; and then *The Fortunata* moved with the tide and slid silently out towards the wide open sea. The journey had begun.

It was dusk when they filed down below. Everyone was aware that there was no going back.

CHAPTER 6

Setting Sail

ON THAT FIRST NIGHT AT SEA there were songs and stories, and by agreement no sad ones, and marvellous tales of emigrants who had become millionaires and had fine clothes and houses now. It was a night to be good-hearted and to try and think of the future, not of the past.

The Fortunata pushed her way through the tranquil seas with darkness all around. The music from below broke the stillness and up on deck the sailors on watch tapped their feet in time, knowing well that though the passengers were in fine fettle the first few days out, time would cure that.

Squashed up with Mary and Nellie on the hard planks with two blankets shared between them and using her old shawl as a pillow, Peggy found it impossible to sleep. There was the constant sound of tossing and turning, of old men groaning and women whispering prayers under their breath – not forgetting the snorers and night walkers. All night Peggy dozed in and out of a fitful sleep. At this rate she would be exhausted by the time they finally reached America.

The next morning it was hot, stuffy and smelly down

below. If only they could open a window and let in some cool air and some light. Already the Atlantic ocean had made sure that nearly three-quarters of the passengers were ill. Both Mary and little Nellie were retching and vomiting. The women and children seemed to get it worst. Nell Molloy said a prayer of thanks for having had the sense to bring the tin bucket.

Peggy lay on her side in the bunk. 'I won't get sick! I won't get sick!' she tried to tell herself, just before she did. She felt clammy and sweaty, and her mouth was dry. Sea-sickness was worse than anything she had ever imagined. She would even have considered jumping overboard if she had been strong enough to get up on deck. Cold sweat and nausea wafted over her, wave after wave, almost to the rhythm of the sea. No one had prepared Peggy for this. She lay still on the bunk for two days, the constant motion attacking her. She could only keep down a few drops of water. Peggy felt such pity for the mothers of little ones trying to manage. The sea was rough and choppy, and clamoured against the boat, trying to seep in. I want to go home! was the thought in her mind every minute.

On the fourth day Peggy could just about sit up. She felt sticky and filthy, but at least the awful rocking feeling had gone. Bill Harvey, a large jovial man, was the kindest of the sailors and when he judged a few of the unfortunate passengers were over the worst of the sickness, he brought them up on top to sit in the fresh breeze. With the aid of a rough damp towel they were able to clean themselves up a bit. Even an hour away from the sourness below was heaven. Overhead the sun blazed. The cook and two assistants were busy stirring up a mess of pork and beans. The smell assaulted Peggy's senses, but she forced back the feeling of sickness and looked around the upper deck.

The sailors' quarters, which they'd heard were not much better than their own, were up at the top end and over them were the captain's rooms. Outside his door was a big basket full of hens who kept up an enormous racket. Hearing the captain barking orders at his cabin boy, Bill sharply ordered the passengers down below again. The captain wanted them out of the way as much as possible.

Nell was busy looking after the children. She had only had a mild dose of sea-sickness but still she didn't look well. The bell rang and the one cooked meal of the day was ready.

Peggy refused the lunch when Nell offered her some, and she passed it down to Thomas and Tim who were always starving. She sat on her bunk and nibbled one of the dry oatcakes Eily had baked for her. A girl stood near the bunk watching her eat. Her green eyes had smudges of grey under them but her smile was wide and friendly. Peggy patted the space beside her. The girl hopped up.

'I'm Sarah, Sarah Connolly.' She grinned.

'Peggy O'Driscoll from Castletaggart.'

They both reached out at the same time to shake hands. Peggy began to giggle, realising what a sight they both were.

'Were you sick too?' asked Peggy.

Sarah nodded. 'Really bad. I wanted to die.'

'Are you on your own?'

'No, I'm with my two older brothers, over there. James is seventeen and John is sixteen.'

Her brothers were sitting at the table, stuffing themselves with the pork and beans.

'I'm fifteen,' smiled Sarah. She was small and her thin curly black hair framed a slightly crooked face. But when she smiled her whole self lit up.

'I'm thirteen, and I'm sort of on my own. My brother Michael was meant to come too but he got a job,' sighed Peggy, 'though I have the Molloys, a family from Castletaggart.'

'Is Castletaggart a nice place?' asked Sarah.

Peggy had to concentrate hard on the wooden edge of the bunk. She didn't trust herself to speak.

'Castletaggart is the best place in the world. My two old great-aunts had a shop there ...'

Hours later they were still chatting, sitting side-by-side on the bunk, sharing the ups and downs of their lives. Sarah's family had been evicted from their farm during the Great Famine. They all moved to the local workhouse and that's where she grew up. Her mother died there and her father was too confused ever to leave the place. A month ago almost half of all the inhabitants were offered free passage to Boston. There was nothing left for Sarah and her brothers to do but take it and try and start a new life.

'I'm not sad leaving, Peggy,' Sarah declared. 'I'm not leaving anyone behind. I know my father is still there, but in his mind we all died long ago. For the last year or so he could hardly recognise us.'

'Oh, Sarah, how sad!' said Peggy.

'I want a new start, Peggy. Come on, we'll get a bit of exercise. Let's walk up and down,' urged the older girl.

Peggy lowered herself from the bunk. She still felt a

bit dizzy. They passed the crowded centre tables. The one near Peggy's bunk was the women's. Every bit of seating was used. The children had the run of the bunks to play in. There wasn't much space to walk, but at least when you had a friend to chat to it wasn't so bad!

CHAPTER 7

The Storm

GRADUALLY PEGGY GOT HER APPETITE BACK. Then like the other passengers she was starving most of the time. She nibbled the oatcakes sparingly, each mouthful a reminder of home and what once had been. The sea was getting rougher and rougher. It was best to stay on the bunk.

Sarah had her hands full, as one of her brothers was badly sea-sick and demanding constant attention.

'I'll talk to you later, Peggy! It's just that John needs me now.'

Nell Molloy tried to cheer her up but most of her gossip involved husbands or babies or women's complaints. She treated Peggy the same as her own children and told her to 'run off and play' when she was talking to the other women.

'There's a storm blowing, mark my words,' announced Nell.

An enormous swell of waves pushed against the side

of the ship. The motion was becoming unsteady. No meal was served.

Bill Harvey shouted down to them all: 'Stay in your bunks. Women, mind those children and try to tie up your belongings. We're in for gale-force winds and the eye of a storm.'

Left on their own in the gloom down below, panic began to spread among the passengers. Sea water seeped through the boards and covered the floor. As soon as the wind began to howl the children started to cry. The ship rocked from side to side. Everyone held on tight to the sides of the bunks.

'Stay where you are!' yelled the men. The huge water barrel broke from its holding and bashed against the lower bunks, all the fresh water spilling into the salt water. Broken oatcakes floated on it. Within an hour the whole of steerage was flooded.

Three small children were flung from the lower bunk into the water. The water shifted and swirled around them as they cried for help. Broken pieces of wood and storage tins and barrels crashed against the walls. Everyone was shouting.

'Save them! Save them!'

Sarah's brother, James Connolly, and the children's father tried to work their way to them. They were flung violently from side to side. The little girl was screaming and clinging on to the leg of a table. Her brother kept trying to stand, but slipped time after time. The two men finally managed to grab them both and hoist them up on to an upper bunk.

'Everyone up in the top bunks,' shouted the children's father. A mad scramble followed. James was frantically feeling round in the water for the third child. Finally he pulled the little two-year-old from under the water. A hush fell on the passengers. Once James lifted him up to the outstretched hands waiting to grasp him, the child began to cough and choke, and water poured from his lungs and mouth.

The men pounded against the battened-down hatches. 'Let us up on deck. We'll be drowned like rats down here,' they shouted. 'We're not criminals!'

All their pleas were lost in the screaming winds and mountainous waves that battered *The Fortunata*.

Mary Molloy was flung like a doll against the bunk. Her face was cut and her arm hung limp from her side, broken.

'Pray, my pets. Pray to God. He's the only one can save us now,' urged Nell.

No matter how she hung on, Peggy could feel herself being torn from the bunk every time the ship heaved. She clung to the side of her bunk, terrified of the blackness below. Suddenly she was in it! She gulped down mouthfuls of the salt water. It almost choked her, and stung her eyes and filled her nostrils. In the darkness she felt for the edge of a bunk and tried to pull herself up. Her arms and body were too heavy for her. Then Sarah and James were dragging her up towards them. She was freezing cold and her teeth were chattering.

'It's all right, Peggy, we've got you,' said Sarah comfortingly.

Peggy shut her eyes, and shivers ran through her. Sarah held her hand tightly. Wave after wave smashed against the sides of the ship. Water was coming down on them from above too. A huge cracking sound came from the top deck.

'Don't let it be the main mast,' prayed John and James.

The whisper of the 'Our Father' began, and one by one more and more voices joined in. Finally Peggy fell asleep with the words of the prayer ringing in her ears. She dreamt of Michael sitting on a big white horse galloping across a green field.

* * *

'Get up! Get up, Peggy. It's all over. The storm is over.' Sarah was awake beside her.

Peggy's head felt muzzy and every bone in her body ached. But the ship was calm at last. Men, women and children began to stir in the upper bunks. Their clothes and blankets were sodden. Favourite possessions lay smashed and floating in the water beneath them.

James was standing with a crowd of men trying to get the captain to open the hatch. Peggy climbed down to the lower bunk and crept along till she got to the Molloys. Tim was crying.

'Are you all right, Nell?'

'I think I'm still in one piece,' joked the woman. 'The children are all half-dead with the fright and the cold.'

Peggy felt a shudder of relief run through her.

'It's all right, Peggy pet. We've all had a close escape.'

'How's Mary's arm?'

'Broken, most like, but broken bones mend.'

An hour later everyone was up on deck. The sailors were tired too – they had been doing their utmost to keep the ship afloat. The main sail had been battered and torn and the masts needed repairing. One sailor had been washed overboard at the height of the storm. Blankets were spread out to dry. A woman was wailing that she'd lost her baby.

A member of the crew appeared with the passenger list and called out the names. The baby and an old man were the only people missing. The crew found them when they were baling out the lower deck. Both had slipped under the water and drowned. At midday everyone huddled together as the captain read a few prayers from his Bible over them.

The two bodies, wrapped in blankets, were lifted up on deck, one large and the other – oh so small! Horrified, Peggy clenched her eyes shut as the two bundles were tossed overboard. Sarah sobbed out loud and James hid her face against his chest. The baby's mother screamed and screamed. All of a sudden she made a run to the side of the ship as if she was going to throw herself overboard after the child – but her husband and another man caught hold of her just in time. Her sobbing and moaning continued on and on. Peggy stared, fascinated and disgusted, as the waves washed over the first grey floating packet. Soon it begin to sink. The smaller bundle bobbed in the eddy of the ship as if reluctant to disappear. Peggy didn't know why but she began to cry too, crying for an old man and a little baby she never knew.

CHAPTER 8

The Long Voyage

FIVE, STINKING, ROTTEN, smelly, disgusting weeks. Peggy had thirty-five straws – well, parts of straws – one for each day, clustered together in a small pile. Every morning and every evening she counted them. Thirty-five days on this festering bit of wood they called a ship. Find your fortune – start a new life – go to a land of promise! It felt as if a joke was being played on them, and at times Peggy was so angry she could have strangled someone – but who? – with her bare hands. Cramped in her bunk on *The Fortunata* with two of the Molloy children leaning up against her, Peggy urged herself to stay calm, stay well – to survive and get to America. Only a few more straws to add to the pile and then a new life lay ahead.

'Slops time,' shouted a sailor, opening the hatch. A glorious waft of fresh air flooded the lower deck. Mothers shook sleeping children and urged them to draw in the air.

Peggy looked over at Mrs Molloy. She looked sick, and one of the younger children lay beside her, ill now with cabin fever because of the stuffy conditions. She nodded to Peggy.

Peggy wrinkled her nose and grabbed the handle of the very full bucket. She tightened her nostrils and clenched her lips – it was best not to think about its contents but just concentrate on getting up the rickety steps and on to the top deck to empty the whole damn lot over the side.

'It's breezy on top, so take care which way it blows,' joked a sailor.

Peggy stood on the sloping deck, pretending to be trying to guess which way the wind was blowing. The waves were lashing against the side of the ship. As the clouds moved in the sky, the water spread all around like a blue and green blanket. In some parts the sea was so green it was like a small field and in others it was so dark it was almost black. This was her third time up on top this week. She gulped in the air, letting it fill her lungs. The wind caught her hair and lashed it wildly to one side – she hoped some of the bugs would get blown away too. She imagined them being blown from her clothes and into the vast expanse of nothingness that lay all around.

A vision of her great-aunt beating the parlour carpet as it hung over the washing line fell like a shadow over her. Blow the cobwebs away – that's what Nano would say.

'Hurry up, lass, it's time to get back down again.'

Peggy slowly emptied the bucket and stood looking around the ship. Her ears picked up the cackling of the captain's hens in their large wicker case.

'Those old hens are better treated than ourselves,' she muttered.

The sailor who was leading her back to the hatch

snapped, 'That may be, my dear, but one of those feath-
ered chickens will have its neck wrung by midday.'

'Birds cooped up in a cage, just like us,' said Peggy.

The sailor pushed the man behind her who stumbled
towards the steps. The crew had strict instructions not to
let anyone dally up on top, as the captain lived in fear of
the passengers protesting at their treatment.

It took a few minutes for Peggy to get used to the
gloom down below in steerage after the bright sunlight.
There was a dreadful stench. Then she blinked and took
a deep breath. She went over and bent down close to
Nell Molloy.

'Are you all right, Nell?'

'Any land yet, pet?' croaked the woman.

Peggy shook her head. She went down to the water
barrel and brought a tin mugful back to the patient.

'Come up here and give your mother a rest,' she said
to the children and patted the bunk.

All the children were getting fractious. Down at the
other end of the deck ten or more spindly little tots were
playing hide-and-seek.

'Think of your mother,' whispered Peggy.

She got her Bible out from under her shawl and
opened it. The favourite story was from the Book of
Genesis. Peggy smiled as she began to read about
Noah's Ark. Some of the words were too difficult for
her, but she skipped over them. She knew the story so
well. The children's mouths opened in awe at the
bravery of Noah and his family, and they tried to
imagine all those animals too. Little Nellie wondered
if it was as crowded or smelly on the ark as it was on
The Fortunata. They all loved the part when the dove

brought back an olive branch.

'Will the captain send out a dove to see if we're in America?' asked Nellie, enchanted with the idea.

An hour later the smell of cooking wafted down from above. At least the captain would provide some rations today. Peggy was down to her last few pieces of oatcake which were now hardened and dirty. Some of the men and women brightened up, stretched and began to walk up and down for exercise before their only meal of the day was served.

Peggy left the children and crossed to the row of bunks on the other side. Sarah Connolly was still fast asleep. Her black curls clung damply to her cheeks and Peggy noticed how long her black eyelashes were.

'Sarah, it's me,' whispered Peggy, hoping that Sarah wasn't beginning to get cabin fever like so many of the others. Sarah yawned, grinned at Peggy and got up. Then they too walked back and forth, making all kinds of plans for when they got to America.

CHAPTER 9

America

'LAND AHEAD!' THE SHOUT went up. Seagull cries filled the air. The sailors, who had been sullen and hostile, now began to whistle and seemed more relaxed. No matter how wretched and worn out they were, journey's end was in sight. An extra meaty stew was served and a full water barrel brought down below.

Peggy was nervous with excitement, but she couldn't help but worry about Nell. Nell continued to refuse food and when Peggy dampened a cloth to wipe her hands and face she could feel how high her temperature was. Little Tim was whingey and cranky and wouldn't let Peggy coax him to play. He lay near his mother, content to be still and quiet.

The next morning, much to everyone's surprise, the captain came half-way down the steps of steerage. A bell clanged for attention, and a hush descended, broken only by a baby squalling. Eager eyes turned towards the captain.

'As you may have guessed, we are in American waters at the moment and later today will arrive at the east coast of America and our destination, the port of Boston. We have had a good passage.' A mumble of dissent floated in the air. He continued: 'Before our arrival there are certain things to be done. It is likely that a doctor or medical committee may come on board to inspect all passengers and judge if they are fit for entry. Bedding and so on must be cleaned up and everything must be in order and ship-shape.' As quick as a wink he turned and disappeared up on deck before a hundred questions could be asked.

Once the hatch shut a strange silence fell on all below. Peggy's eyes welled up with tears, she felt so happy and yet so anxious. Sarah was just the same. What would happen to Nell and little Tim, Peggy wondered. No one could look at the sick and ailing who lay in their bunks and face the questions in their eyes. Would they be sent all the way back?

An hour later the hatch opened and six sailors came down. They dragged the old straw off the bunks, scattered the deck with dry sand, then one of them swept the filthy floor with a large brush. The festering straw and dirt were shovelled into old sacks and lugged up on deck. Two more sailors came down and began to pull the mouldy dirt-covered blankets from the bunks. Two or three old women tried vainly to grab their blankets and wrap them around themselves.

'You won't get this, you thief,' screamed one as the sailor none-too-gently unrolled her from it.

The blankets were tied with hanks of rope and brought up on top too. Peggy managed to run quickly up the steps just in time to see the sailors catch the sacks and fling them out to sea. Then they kicked the bundles of blankets over. The dirt from the blankets began to spread in the water and then, as they filled up and got heavier, they began to sink under the foam like giant purple jellyfish.

Later, buckets and scrubbing brushes and large tablets of soap were sent below and the women began to scrub the tables and floor. The hatch was left open and the breeze did its best to blow the smell of sickness and staleness away. The women's eyes were red with shame and anger. They scrubbed with ferocity and temper and let the crude heavy soap wash their dirty hands and arms. A few of them threw the harsh soapy water on their faces and quickly dried themselves on their shawls. They felt hurt and resentful, thinking of all the times they had begged for soap and water for washing, especially after the storm and sickness, and had been refused.

Peggy felt a burning rage within her. Although busy, she cursed the captain and his crew for this outrage committed against her people. She filled two tin mugs with the scalding water and called the young Molloys over to her. Sarah laughed at her as with a bit of torn rag she tried furiously to scrub the grime and dirt off their young faces and hands.

'Stay still,' she shouted as they squirmed and squealed like young piglets. She felt it was the least she could do for Nell and her family.

Up on top you could definitely see the coastline with its sweeping curves and bays bathed in a beautiful golden sunshine. Whether down below or up above, everyone sat quiet and still as they sailed nearer and nearer. They had actually managed to make it all the way from Ireland to America! And then came a sudden jolt after the captain had ordered, 'Drop anchor.'

Why had they stopped? No one seemed to know. They noticed a large boat rowing out to them. It kept coming until it reached the side of *The Fortunata*. Three people climbed up the ladder and boarded the ship. Down below in her bunk Peggy could hear the hum of conversation as they walked all around the upper deck. Then Bill Harvey came down the steps.

'Now, a bit of hush, please. We have visitors – a doctor, a nursing sister and an official from Boston Port Authority, so the captain asks you to co-operate with them as we all want to get landed as soon as possible.'

Peggy felt scared. Sometimes in the last few weeks she had been dizzy and light-headed and she felt her heart thumping in her chest and a shortness of breath. What if they detected it too?

Some of the men looked nonchalant while the women looked scared. They whispered to the children and pinched their cheeks to give them a bit of colour.

They formed lines and made their way to the tables where they took it in turn to sit down opposite the nurse. The doctor sat at the far end of the table and examined those the nurse passed on to him.

The official walked around the bunks with Bill Harvey, looking at anyone who was bedridden. Peggy stood nervously beside Nell and her family at their bunk. Tim had fallen into a heavy sleep, but nothing could hide how white and listless he was. Peggy and Mary had done their best to brush and plait Nell's hair and tidy her up. She was pale and clammy to touch. The official noted the invalid and child in the bunk awaiting the doctor's attention. Bill motioned to Peggy to get in line with the rest.

'Name?' asked the nurse.

'Peggy O'Driscoll,' gulped Peggy.

'Age, and alone or accompanied?'

What should she say? Sarah reckoned that the families of those who were sick would not be let land. If she said she was with Nell, would they send her back to Ireland? But if she was too young would she be let in?

'I ... I'm thirteen years of age and I am, I suppose, on my own,' answered Peggy, hoping she'd said the right thing.

The nurse began to prod her all over. 'Any cough, any sweating or fever?'

Peggy shook her head and prayed to God the nurse wouldn't feel her heart jumping wildly. The nurse seemed satisfied. However the doctor called her towards him. He looked at her eyes and her throat and felt her neck and then he listened to her heart. Peggy tried to slow down her breathing. She looked at his eyes, waiting for the worst.

'Well, young lady, nothing the matter that fresh air and a bit of good food won't put to rights. Good luck and find your fortune.'

Peggy ran over and climbed up on Sarah's bunk. They hugged each other.

'I'm fine, Sarah,' laughed Peggy.

'Me too,' smiled Sarah, 'but he said I'm not to do much heavy work.'

'What about the Molloys?' murmured Peggy. She felt guilty about denying that she was with them. She and Sarah glanced over to the other side of the ship. The doctor and official were busy discussing the patient and her child. As soon as they moved off, Peggy ran over. Nell's eyes were closed and she was totally worn out with the effort of trying to appear well.

'Peggy, we have to go to an island with a special hospital place for a few weeks till Mammy's better. All of us together. I think it's like a workhouse.' Mary's eyes were round with alarm.

Peggy bent down and sat on the wooden edge beside her.

'Did they say it's a workhouse, Mary?'

'No, not for sure.'

'Well, then, it's not the workhouse. It's a place to make your Mam and brother better and help look after you all. Isn't it a lot better than being sent straight back home on the boat like some we've heard of,' said Peggy comfortingly. 'You'll still be in America.' Peggy tried to hide her own dismay at the thought of being separated from such a good, kind family. She would miss them so much.

The next few hours passed in a frenzy of excitement and nerves. The hatch remained firmly closed. They felt like animals on the way to the market to be sold. Then suddenly the daylight flooded in and the sick began to walk or be lifted up on deck to leave for the hospital on Deer Island.

'Oh, Nell, will you be all right?'

'Peggy, don't be fretting. There's life in the old dog yet! The only thing I'm worried about is himself. Will you find him and tell him what's happened and where we are?' begged Nell.

'I'll find him. Don't worry, Nell.'

Peggy hugged her and then she kissed Mary, Tom, Tim and little Nell in turn.

A silence descended on the whole of steerage as the sick were taken off. Then the ship began to move again. Peggy sat listlessly over the empty bunk. In an hour she would be gone from this ship. It was hard to believe that in another two months another girl might sit here, setting sail too for America.

'Boston! America!' a shout went up.

Peggy joined the mad scramble and pushed her way up on deck to get a good view of their new home. They sailed slowly into the East Bay. All around them ships shoved their way in and out of the busy crowded harbour. The magnificent city of Boston lay spread out in front of them.

'We made it,' laughed Sarah. 'Peggy, can you believe it! Isn't it beautiful? Look at those buildings and all the ships.'

Compared to Queenstown it was enormous. All the harbours and bays jutted out into the ocean, and they could see huge long streets flanked by tall stone buildings. There were fine houses in every direction. The dots in the distance got nearer and nearer – soon Peggy could read the names on the buildings and see the bonnets and shawls the women wore.

She took out her counting straws. Slowly she unclenched her fist – and forty pieces of broken straw caught the wind and blew out over the water. In a few seconds they had disappeared.

The Fortunata was getting ready to dock. On one side were large warehouses. Crates and boxes were stacked neatly outside them and gangs of dockers moved these from place to place. Two or three other large ships which were being boarded lay nearby. *The Fortunata* finally managed to find a space, and Peggy and the others tried to keep out of the sailors' way as they cast ropes to the waiting hands on the wharf.

In next to no time the gangplank had been set across and one by one the passengers began to leave the ship. Peggy hoped that she would never put a foot on *The Fortunata* or any ship like it for the rest of her life.

CHAPTER 10

First Foot Forward

CARRYING THEIR BUNDLES, Peggy and Sarah took a few wobbly steps away from the ship. A small cheer went up for everyone who disembarked as they put their feet on solid American soil for the first time. A crowd of people stood on the wharf waiting to welcome the arrivals. Such hugging and crying and joking! Peggy envied those who had someone to meet them and welcome them.

Young fellows of nine or ten ran in and out among the crowd pretending to give a hand with luggage, but trying in the process to lead people towards a particular boarding house. These were the runners, sent out to get new customers whenever a ship landed. Peggy had been well warned about them and kept a tight grip on her bag and bundle. The whole quayside was covered with trunks and boxes, all being guarded by the new arrivals. Peggy's eyes were blinded by all that was going on and kept being lured by the large buildings in the distance and the busy streets. She had to force herself to scan the crowds to try and spot Daniel Molloy.

The ship had emptied and now the sailors were going ashore. She noticed a man who made his way to the gangplank. He looked so worried. He was smaller than Nell had described. His cheeks were ruddy and he wore a shabby-looking tweed suit with a clean white shirt. He paced up and down, searching for someone. Peggy left Sarah and made her way towards him. She pulled at his jacket and he turned to her.

'Mr Molloy, is it?'

'Yes, lassie. Can I help you?' he asked, looking totally puzzled.

'No, Mr Molloy. But I've a message for you from Mrs Molloy.'

'The Mrs! You've a message from herself! Where in heaven's name is she and all my dotes?'

'She's safe, but herself and Tim were sick so they all had to get off a few hours before us and go to the hospital on Deer Island instead. Lots of passengers went.' Peggy's eyes took in the fear and anxiety in his face. 'Honest, Mr Molloy, she's been sick with fever, but they've doctors there to look after them.'

Dan Molloy's cheerful smile had crumpled in dismay and he took a dirty-looking hanky from his pocket and blew his nose.

'You're the grand girl to seek me out, lassie, and I'm grateful for it as the last half hour I've been near mad with worrying about them all.'

Peggy nodded, understanding his disappointment.

'I'm Peggy O'Driscoll from Castletaggart and Mary

and I went to the same school and I've shared the whole journey with Mrs Molloy and all of them. She took good care of me and I'm lucky to have such friends.'

There and then Dan Molloy hugged her.

'Isn't it lovely after two years to meet a friend from the old home! I'm settled the far side of Boston and work in a big timberyard and have lodgings in a street nearby.' He stopped. 'Have you a place to stay or anyone to stay with?'

Peggy made a quick decision. Dan Molloy was a good man, but he had enough to worry about with Nell and the children. She had a little money and anyway Sarah was waiting for her.

'It's all right, Mr Molloy, but thanks for asking anyway. My friend Sarah and I are going to get somewhere together.'

He clasped her hand warmly and told her his address quickly before he moved off to find someone who could tell him how to get to Deer Island.

Peggy ran back to Sarah who was busy trying to wrench a battered suitcase from a snotty-nosed brat. Once her brother John came into view the kid ran off.

Peggy suddenly felt lonely and tired and a lot like crying. She sat on her bundle. John and James were going to lodge in a place for working men and were trying to sort out something for their younger sister and for Peggy. John picked up the case and Peggy's bundle and led them towards a crowd clustering around a large woman who had positioned herself in front of a small 'baccy' shop. She was sitting on some kind of fold-up chair and a placard lay resting under the window sill announcing her identity: Mrs Margaret Halligan, landlady and proprietor of the Shamrock Agency for the Employment of Young Ladies. In brackets underneath 'Just like a mother' was proclaimed in green writing. Four girls from the ship stood to one side of her. James led Sarah and Peggy over. He took one of the woman's cards, read it and put it in his pocket.

'What do you think, Peggy?' asked Sarah.

Peggy shrugged.

'It seems like the kind of place we could go.' Sarah was all excited.

'Will you help us find jobs?' Peggy asked the woman.

She laughed. 'The finest jobs in Boston!'

Sarah and Peggy made a quick decision and joined the girls beside her.

John and James said their goodbyes, then disappeared into the crowd, with promises to come and visit Sarah the following Sunday. The gangs of people had begun to disperse and the waterfront to empty. There were shouts of 'Good luck' all around.

Margaret Halligan stood up and a young fellow folded up the chair and carried the placard.

'Now, girls, follow me to Number 49, Empire Hill, the best home for young ladies in all Boston,' she instructed, and marched ahead.

They walked slowly, the six girls trying to gape at the streets. They passed the magnificent City Hall. Mrs Halligan pointed out the huge markets and food hall beside it. Broad-leafed shady trees lined the streets, which were wide and clean. Mrs Halligan kept up a commentary as they went along. Soon they came to an area with narrow, winding streets, and Mags told them the names of the streets they were passing and which

shops were good or bad. Most of them were too bam-
boozled to take any of it in. They kept firmly in line behind
the large gold and black bonnet and layers of skirt and petticoat of Mags Halligan, the mother of them all! Arriving
at Number 49, Peggy felt her spirits sink. It was a large
stone house with ramshackle steps leading to a brown
door. A green shamrock made of wood was nailed to the
plasterwork at the side.

Inside the door the scent of lavender polish and beeswax fought a battle against the smell of corned beef and
greens coming from the kitchen. A maid about the same
age as Peggy led them upstairs to a long narrow room.
Opening the door, Peggy was surprised to see more
bunks.

'Get two bunks, Sarah, quickly!' shouted Peggy.
They both made a dash for the one in the corner, near
the window. Peggy took the top bunk.

'Ye's can all have a rest and Mrs Halligan will be up to
talk to ye when she's ready.' The girl, who looked
weary, opened the large clumsy wardrobe and told
them to deposit their belongings there, not on or under
the beds as it caused dust.

Peggy stretched out straight away. She was amazed
at herself. She would have put a bet on a few days ago
that the minute she'd leave the ship all she would do
was run around Boston and explore every bit of it, and
yet here she was lying in another bunk. Her legs could
not get used to dry land and she felt as if she could sleep
for a month. Sarah was already snoring softly.

Empire Hill, Boston, America – it didn't matter where
in the world you were, a bed was a bed and sleep was
sleep ...

* * *

'Up you get, my fine ladies,' boomed Mags Halligan a few hours later. A large starched white pinafore was stretched over her ample frame and a thickly coiled clump of auburn hair sat on top of the fair-skinned face with its broad cheekbones and twinkling green eyes.

Peggy and Sarah rubbed the sleep from their eyes and did their best to look attentive and alert.

'There'll be no grub served until you are all boiled and cleaned and scrubbed. I'll not have filth or dirt in my house, so no messing and down to the washroom.'

Nancy, the young maid they had already met, led them down the corridor two by two to a large tiled room where there were two baths which belched out steam and heat.

Peggy and Sarah were both forced into the almost scalding hot water. Every bit of them had to be cleaned from top to toe. They scrubbed themselves with a thick soap which smelt of lily and once Nancy had looked at their heads, a foul-smelling shampoo was rubbed into their scalps which made Peggy feel like her brain would burst. Her eyes were streaming and her skin was so hot and pink she felt like a boiled lobster. She began to wonder if she had fallen into the hands of some crazed woman, when Nancy told her to 'Get up out of it', and tossed her a large grey bath-sheet to dry herself off. Sarah was coughing and spluttering in between laughing at how funny Peggy looked.

They were then led back up the hall to Mrs Halligan's room. Sarah was told to wait while Peggy went in. Mags

Halligan looked Peggy up and down and Peggy could feel herself go crimson with embarrassment. Mrs Halligan then told her to sit in a chair while she inspected her hair, lifting it up with the thin end of a comb.

'Another one, Nancy. Fetch me the scissors.'

Nancy passed the large grey shears to Mags, who then clipped about nine inches off Peggy's hair. It fell to the ground and lay on top of the hair from the girls before her.

Nancy next started to fine-comb Peggy's head. After a few minutes she passed the comb to Peggy to continue.

'Get the rest of the nits out yourself, then put these on.' She passed Peggy a pile of clothes, all well washed and worn.

Looking at herself in a mirror, Peggy could not believe the pale-faced stick of a girl she had turned into during the few weeks at sea. But she did admit she liked being clean and fresh and rid of the constant plague of lice and itching that had afflicted her from the minute she boarded *The Fortunata*.

Downstairs in the kitchen the cook ladled out a thick oxtail soup, followed by corned beef served with a mound of potatoes and a bowl of parsnips and carrots. It was like food from heaven and they all wolfed it down.

Mags Halligan joined them then and plumped a large fruit soda down in front of them. She passed a mug of milky tea to each of them, along with a slice of the soda bread. For one second Peggy could almost imagine she was at home.

Mags startled them by laughing out loud to herself. 'Twenty-five years ago I came out here with my sister

Bridget,' she declared, 'just like the lot of you here –
green and stupid and scared – and now look at me! A
fine lady, respectable, with a house of my own and a
good business which is growing day by day. I have six
rooms let out and I look after my lodgers well. Then
there is the likes of yourselves who I take in and help
settle and find jobs for. I know what the fine ladies of
Boston want. I've had twenty years of sculleries and
pantries and kitchens and downstairs and upstairs.
Play your cards right with me and you'll land on
your feet. I'll get positions for you all if you follow
my rules. No one likes a dirty maid, so it's essential to
look clean and presentable. Also, I know what it's
like to arrive in a strange country, worn out and hungry. I'll feed ye and keep ye for a few days to get ye
started.'

Peggy looked at Mags in admiration. What a woman,
and such a big heart!

'And what do you get out of all this?' questioned Josie
O'Donnell, a large red-faced girl.

Peggy and Sarah winked at each other. Trust Josie.
She was always the first to want to know what was
going on in steerage – still, she had a nerve to talk to
Mags like that.

'It's good to see one of you with a brain in her head,'
laughed Mags. 'I hope to get places for you all as soon as
possible, but meanwhile there's work to be done here.
Domestic employment is what most of you will find,
though there are the factory jobs for those that want
them – machining and sewing. Naturally you'll pay me
for your keep and later there's a fee for finding a job. Is
that all clear now?'

She looked around at the six eager faces, all wondering what lay ahead of them.

CHAPTER 11

Skivvy

'IT'S A GREAT OPPORTUNITY, Miss, so mind you don't let me down.' Mrs Halligan stared straight at Peggy.

Peggy was to work as a maid in a boarding house for men. She tried to smile. She should be delighted to land a job so soon, but she was nervous of being on her own and of leaving Sarah.

'Do you think I'll do all right?'

'Peggy O'Driscoll, you're a stubborn mule like myself. But you're as bright as a button too. Helping to run a boarding house – this way you'll be learning the ropes,' declared Mags reassuringly.

'I suppose so!' shrugged Peggy.

'Now, run and get your belongings and say goodbye to the others and I'll bring you down the street to Mona Cavendish's in an hour or so. It's not at the end of the earth, you know!'

In what seemed no time, Peggy found herself standing outside a gloomy wooden house in a narrow, mean, crowded street about ten minutes' walk away from Mags Halligan's.

'Well, I'm not saying, Peggy, that Mrs Cavendish is

the best landlady in Boston, but then she's not the worst. She is from Liverpool originally. Anyways, it's a start.'

A red-faced woman, her hair in two greasy coils at the side of her head, opened the door.

'Well, is this the girl then?' she questioned.

Mrs Halligan nodded. 'Fresh off the boat, Mona, but a good worker.'

'Well, I hope she's better than the last one!'

Peggy stood, filled with misery, looking into the grimy hallway. Every instinct told her to run, but instead she said goodbye to Mags and followed the other woman inside.

'Now, Peggy, you follow the instructions I give you and we'll get on fine and dandy.'

The kitchen was cluttered and untidy. A halfprepared meat pie was sitting in the middle of the table.

'Just look at the state the last one left me in,' said Mrs Cavendish, 'and now there's another greenhorn to train!'

Peggy was told to brush up the peelings and dirt that littered the stone floor, and she watched out of the corner of her eye as Mona Cavendish deftly finished off the pastry and slid the pie into the huge oven.

'Come on, Peggy, and I'll show you what's what! This is where they all eat.' Two wooden tables were crowded into a long narrow room, lit by a window overlooking the street. 'No food allowed in the rooms, you mind! It would only bring rats and such like.'

Another room was stuffed to bursting with a couch and oddments of chairs. It was heavy with the smell of stale tobacco. The curtains were yellow and hung limply

at a closed window that overlooked the back yard. Upstairs on two floors were five rooms, each containing
three or four beds. The beds themselves were practically
on top of each other. Hooks protruded from a wall at the
end and a medley of clothes hung from them. Peggy
wrinkled her nose against the smell of stale sweat that
swamped her.

'Each room to be checked every day and swept out,
with special care paid to under the beds – I'm telling
you, nobody would believe the things I've found under
those beds!'

'Yes, Mrs Cavendish,' murmured Peggy, vowing to
herself to open the window of every room before she
even touched anything.

They passed a closed door. 'That's my room,' the
owner nodded.

Peggy wondered where she herself was meant to
sleep. 'Are there any more rooms?'

'No, Peggy, that's as many as does. Most of the time
it's full.'

Back downstairs Peggy was still waiting to discover
where she would sleep. The woman marched through
the kitchen and pointed to a small cramped room beside
the scullery. It should really have been a storage room,
but had been turned into a makeshift bedroom with a
narrow pallet bed and the tiniest window that looked
out to an outside water closet.

'It's small, but it's handy.' Mona Cavendish had
turned back towards the kitchen. 'Get your bag and put
your things away. There's a great amount of work to
catch up on.'

With a sinking feeling, Peggy realised she was the

only maid in the place. She was tempted to grab her bag and go back and find *The Fortunata* and beg the captain to take her home. But it was useless. She hadn't enough money to pay for her passage, and God knows how long it would take to work and save for it. Anyway, the thought of such a journey! Nothing could be that bad.

It was late afternoon when Peggy heard the tramp of heavy feet on the wooden floorboards overhead. The lodgers were home. Two massive pots of potatoes were boiled and the meat pie was piping hot. Sweat dripped off Mona Cavendish as both of them carried the food to the packed dining-room. The men cheered when they walked in and some of them winked at Peggy. She was bombarded with questions.

'Yes, from Ireland,' she answered, 'Castletaggart – do you know it? … *The Fortunata.*'

Between them Mona and Peggy managed to make sure that each man had a good share of food on his plate. Giant jugs of milk were brought too. Silence descended as the men began their meal.

Peggy looked around at them. Most were Irish, but a few were from strange-sounding places. Their clothes were grimy and stained and their faces tanned and weather-beaten. All of them worked in building of some kind and their fingernails were encrusted with dirt.

In what seemed only a few seconds the plates were empty and Peggy was set to gather them up and take them back downstairs for washing. Mrs Cavendish prepared four huge pots of tea.

'You wash up down below,' she ordered and left Peggy to it.

Here she was in a crowded house and yet Peggy had

never felt so lonely. It was almost dark when she finished in the kitchen. Some of the men were playing cards in the smoke-filled room. Upstairs others lay stretched out on their beds, reading or writing a letter. Another group had wandered off for a walk.

Peggy thought she had better check with Mrs Cavendish before going to bed, so she knocked timidly at the landlady's bedroom door, and not getting a reply she pushed it in.

'Mrs Cavendish, Mrs Cavendish.'

The woman lay stretched out on the bed in all her clothes with her eyes shut.

'I think everything is just about cleared.'

Mrs Cavendish, half-asleep, began to mutter. 'I'm worn out with all the work, it's no wonder I fell asleep.' Peggy nodded. 'Make sure the place is set for the morning breakfast – you can't send a working man off to build roads and railways and the like on an empty stomach, least that's always been my policy. Anyways, you're done then for the day, so away to your bed.'

Peggy's room was damp despite the warm night air and she tossed and turned on the uncomfortable bed. The only good thing was that she wouldn't hear the constant snoring that went on upstairs. She prayed to Auntie Lena to help her in this awful place. Maybe tomorrow things would be better.

* * *

Her prayers were not answered. With every day things got worse. Mrs Cavendish, who would chat and be friendly one minute, was liable to be like a devil the next, and Peggy's arm was already bruised from the pinches her new mistress inflicted on her.

'Get up, you lazy chit, I'm not paying for you to be lying in bed,' she shouted early in the morning on Peggy's third day, storming into her bedroom and dragging the light blanket off her. She flung her dress at her. 'We've a breakfast to serve!'

By mid-morning every day Mrs Cavendish would disappear either up the town or to bed. Peggy was left to see to everything. At three o'clock the landlady would reappear and if the rooms or hallway were not clean enough or Peggy had forgotten something, she would get a clip on the ear or yet another pinch.

The only good thing was the lodgers. They chatted to Peggy and told her about their families and shared their dreams with her. But they would be there one day and gone a few days later.

'We're building the railways of America,' they'd laugh. 'We'll be millionaires yet.'

Peggy's life seemed grey and miserable in comparison. One or two nights she woke up crying in her sleep. 'I want to go home. God, let me go home. Send me back to Ireland and I'll be good for the rest of my life,' she prayed. She wondered what was happening to Sarah and whether she had got work yet. She longed for her friend.

No miracle happened and when she opened her eyes she was still in the same room, in the same house. Every day seemed like a hundred. Mrs Cavendish seemed to have forgotten about her day off.

'Can I have Thursday off, Mrs Cavendish, please?'

The landlady slurped her early-morning cup of tea.

'No, it doesn't suit this week. When I'm better sorted, Peggy, I'll make it up to you.'

Peggy just about stopped herself crying in front of the woman.

One day there was still no sign of the landlady at four o'clock. Peggy stood in the pale sunlight, looking up the street, watching to see if she could spot her returning. It was time to prepare the dinner. By six o'clock Peggy was frantic. She could hear the men arriving back. She had peeled the potatoes and they lay in water in a big tin bucket.

Big Jim Donovan peered down into the kitchen.

'Lassie, we're getting mighty hungry up here.'

'It'll be ready soon,' she assured him.

Like a whirlwind she put the saucepans on to boil. She searched the pantry and the cold house for some meat. There was nothing.

'What'll I do? What'll I do? What would Eily do?'

She found two dozen eggs and scrambled them with some chopped onion. Then she boiled up a dishful of beans. All the time she was aware of the coughs coming from above and the stamping of feet and banging of forks and spoons on the tables.

One of the younger lads helped her to carry the food up. She was puce with embarrassment and could see the men's faces fall as they realised what their main meal would be. Sweat ran down her back and her hair and forehead were soaked after all her effort. The potatoes at the bottom of the saucepans had turned to a mush whilst the top ones were only half-cooked. There was only a small helping of eggs for each man. When she poured the tea she knew it was long overstewed.

'You could dance a donkey on it, as my old mother would say,' one of the men said jokingly.

Peggy left them to it. At the bottom of the stairs Peggy heard snoring. She followed the sound to Mrs Cavendish's room. The landlady lay under the blankets with her good blouse still on. Her clothes littered the floor.

Peggy stared at her. Up close she could smell something. It was whisky!

A large leg of mutton lay wrapped in white paper and flung in a bloody mess on the bedroom floor. So that's what happened to the dinner, Peggy thought, and she picked it up and brought it downstairs.

In the early hours of the morning, Peggy was woken by a shout:

'Get up, you snivelling little brat.'

She rubbed her eyes, and stared at the woman standing over her. She had expected the landlady to thank her for managing.

'What have you been up to, you stupid girl?'

Peggy blinked. Mona Cavendish's hair hung loose. She looked crazed.

Peggy got up out of the bed. 'Mrs Cavendish, what do you mean? It's the middle of the night!'

The woman dragged Peggy into the kitchen and pointed at the shelves. 'Tell me what you expect me to do. Not an egg left in the house. Do you think I'd send a man off to do a day's work on a piece of bread?'

'But I did my best … they needed something to eat so I boiled up potatoes and scrambled the …'

The woman grabbed Peggy and shook her, and then her fist flew out in a temper and caught Peggy across the mouth. 'Get back to your bed, you little troublemaker!'

Peggy ran to her room and banged the door. Already

blood spattered her shift and lay in blobs on the floor. A few minutes later she could hear steps overhead as Mona Cavendish made her drunken way back upstairs.

Sobs racked Peggy's body and she raced to the kitchen sink to throw cold water on her mouth and face to stop it swelling. Her lip was split and she tasted the blood with her tongue. She felt her jaw and gums tenderly with her fingers. She took her hands away and noticed in the middle of the blood on the floor – her tooth.

'You old rat bag,' she screamed.

Peggy walked around the kitchen muttering to herself. 'You knocked out my tooth – that's *my* tooth.' She sobbed and raged. 'Calm down, calm down,' she urged herself.

Immediately she remembered an old cure of Nano's. She grabbed a small cup, filled it with milk and trying not to touch the tooth, pushed it with the corner of her fingernail into the cup. The milk turned pink. Then she felt the space with the tip of her tongue and, draining the cup, gently lifted out the tooth and pushed it back into its socket. The gum was swollen and bleeding but the tooth seemed to stick to it. She dared not test it with her tongue. After ten minutes she felt it just might stay there.

She walked round and round the kitchen table. Stay or go, stay or go? she wondered.

Suddenly the decision was made. She ran into her bedroom, grabbed her things and shoved them into her bag. She pulled off her shift, threw it in on top, pulled on her dress and wrapped her shawl around herself.

I'll not face another day under that one's roof, she decided.

Soon it would be dawn. She opened the back door and

as silent as a mouse tiptoed through the yard, trying not to trip over the odds and ends that littered it. There was a wooden gate at the bottom of the yard that opened out to a cramped tradesman's delivery lane. The gate was stiff and heavy. She could not open it.

'Open ... open,' Peggy pleaded, pulling as hard as she could.

She gave one final desperate jerk. The bolt flew back and in a flash she was in the lane. It was littered with crates and battered boxes and horse droppings. With wings on her feet she made her escape.

CHAPTER 12

The Runaway

 TWO HOURS LATER, HAVING walked around half of Boston in the early morning light, Peggy found herself sitting on the steps outside Mags Halligan's, hoping for some sign that the household was awake. Every time a stranger came round the corner she was ready to run, in case it was Mona Cavendish coming to fetch her back. She had walked up past the huge market. Early-morning traders were beginning to set up their stalls. It must have been dark when the farmers had left their farms with their produce.

It was only when she went to try and buy a drink for herself that she realised she hadn't been paid yet. She hadn't a cent. She had nowhere to go. The only friends she had were at Number 49, Empire Hill.

'Peggy! Is that you?'

Peggy nearly jumped with fright. Nancy was standing, brush in hand, on the step above her. 'What in heaven's name happened to you? Wait till herself sees you!'

Peggy was afraid to talk too much in case her tooth fell out again.

'Come inside! Come inside!' urged Nancy.

She helped Peggy in and down to the kitchen. There were sounds of movement upstairs, but no one else was up.

'Would you like a cup of tea? They say it's good for shock,' said Nancy.

Peggy nodded.

The other girl put the water on to boil and then disappeared. A few seconds later she came back with Mrs Halligan. The woman was in her nightgown, her hair tumbling half-way down her back. Somehow she looked softer and younger.

Peggy was afraid to look her in the eye. Maybe she'd put her out on the street.

'Well, what's all this to-do about?' she asked. Slowly she walked in front of Peggy, then reached out and tilted her face towards the light. 'Who did this to you, child? Was it one of the men?'

Peggy shook her head. 'It was herself, Mrs Cavendish.'

'That old rip. Picking on a young one like yourself. I'll not have it.'

Peggy wasn't sure if it was relief, but she began to shake from top to bottom.

'Peggy, come on upstairs, you're all done in. Now, away up before the rest of the girls see you.' Mags followed her up the stairs. 'In here, pet.' She led her to a room on its own. 'Get into bed, I'll fix your pillows.'

Peggy crawled into the bed. The mattress was soft and there were crisp sheets and a pink and green striped coverlet.

'I'll be back in a minute, Peggy.'

Mrs Halligan went out.

Hot tears began to roll down Peggy's face, and once she started to cry she couldn't stop. She felt like a little girl again and longed for someone to come and mind her. I hate America, I want to go home. Oh God, just let me go home! she thought.

Mags Halligan stood beside the bed with a bowl and a cloth.

'Let me dab your lip, Peggy, and clean it up a bit. Is it very sore?'

Peggy couldn't answer. She just let the sobs go on and on. The older woman ignored them and cleaned her face gently.

'I'll sit with you for a while,' whispered Mags.

Peggy was ashamed as Mags watched her.

'I'm so lonely,' she stuttered. 'I miss my sister and my brother and my aunt. I miss my friends – I just miss everything about home!'

Mags stroked her hair. With her eyes shut, Peggy could almost make-believe it was Eily sitting beside her.

'Cry, little girl. Let it all out! If you don't cry it will break your heart.'

Peggy stared at Mags. The woman looked tired but kind.

'All of us here have cried, Peggy, believe you me. We all miss our homes and the ones we love. The years pass, we get older, but I don't think it ever goes away.'

'Never?'

'It'll ease, pet. Look at you, Peggy! Lying here half-scared in my house with your lip split and your face puffed and yet I'll tell you those tears will save you.'

'But I don't understand.'

'Just know this – there isn't a girl in this house that

won't shed tears like you've done. It may not be at this time, it may be in six months' time or a year's time or the day she will wed or have her first child. Sometime in her future. But you – you're lucky it has happened so early on. You'll get over it. You're a born survivor.'

Peggy was baffled, but realised that Mags understood in some strange way how she felt.

'Do you want to see the damage?' asked Mags. She held up a small mirror.

Peggy couldn't believe how bad her face looked. Her top lip was split and the whole of her mouth was swollen. The skin under her nose was bruised. It hurt to open her mouth. But at least the tooth was still there!

'Mrs Cavendish knocked my tooth out,' she murmured.

'Was Mona drunk? Was that it?'

'I think so.'

Mags nodded. 'I'd heard rumours, but I wasn't sure.'

'Will she come to make me go back?'

Mags Halligan threw back her head and laughed. 'Let Mona put one foot through my door and she'll have me to deal with. I don't think she'll dare trouble you.'

Peggy yawned. She suddenly realised just how tired she was. Mags kept on talking but Peggy didn't hear a word she said.

Hours later she woke to find Sarah sitting at the end of the bed. 'I'm glad you're back, Peggy, I missed you,' she said.

Peggy grinned ruefully. 'Ow! it's sore!' Her face was stiff and it hurt to talk. 'How are all the others?' she asked.

'The girls have all gone except me. I started at a job in

Goldman's shirt factory. It's not too bad. So I'm a kind of boarder here now until the boys get us a place of our own. They both got work straight away. James is working for the railways and John is helping to build a bank.'

'Did Mrs Halligan tell you what happened?' Peggy asked. Sarah nodded. 'I stuck it out as long as I could and then I knew I had to run away. I didn't even get one cent for all the work I did. Oh, Sarah, I hope I get another job.'

After dinner that evening, Mags Halligan moved Peggy into a small room with Sarah. During the day Peggy helped Nancy with the housework, and as Sarah left for work at seven-thirty in the morning they had hardly any time together.

'Why don't you come and work at Goldman's with me?' Sarah pleaded. 'We'd be together.'

Peggy shook her head. Sarah had told her how crowded and cramped the factory was and about her nasty supervisor, and anyway it wasn't worth the extra money she'd get as that would all go on food and lodgings.

'You know me and sewing,' she said to Sarah, laughing. 'I'd never manage.'

At the end of the week Mrs Halligan told Peggy she had found a new job for her.

'It's in a fine house a few miles outside the city.'

'Will I be the only maid?' Peggy asked.

'No. They have a few other staff, so you won't be lonely and this time there'll be no nonsense. It's a very respectable family called the Rowans that you'll be working for.'

'When will I be starting?'

'I'll take you there tomorrow. The housekeeper is an acquaintance of mine from way back,' said Mrs Halligan.

Sarah hugged her when she heard the good news.

'I'm delighted for you, Peggy, you deserve it! We'll both have good jobs. We'll be well on our way to making our fortune, just wait and see!'

Peggy tried to smile. But she was really anxious about the new job and leaving Sarah and the safety of Number 49 behind.

CHAPTER 13

A Good Capable Girl

IT WAS A SWELTERING DAY. Peggy O'Driscoll stood in the driveway staring in amazement at the enormous house with rounded columns at the front and bright painted shutters on each window.

'Oh, it's beautiful,' she whispered.

'Close your mouth, Peggy, or you'll swallow the flies,' joked Mags Halligan.

The two of them had managed to get a ride in a pony and trap to the suburb of Greenbay. On one side of the curved avenue magnificent mansions stood surrounded by lawns and gardens, each one different, yet beautiful and visible from the road – unlike grand houses at home, Peggy recalled.

Rushton was like a Roman temple. The garden was ablaze with a myriad of summer flowers.

'Oh, Mrs Halligan, I know I'll be happy living in such a wonderful house!' sighed Peggy.

Mrs Halligan stopped suddenly and turned to face her. 'Peggy, this is a society house in a society town. Look at the gardens, go on, have a look around you. Oh yes! you may look at all these beautiful flowers, lilies, roses and orchids, admire them … but do not dare to touch or pick them. You and I are from a different world – it's buttercups and daisies we were raised to. You've got sense in that pretty head of yours, so use it. Be polite and good-mannered – it's what they like – but keep your spirit and dreams secret. A good capable girl is what they want and that's what they'll get.'

Peggy understood what Mags was trying to tell her. Her stomach was in a knot and she felt sick with nerves. Mags knocked on the door. It was opened by a tall middle-aged woman who showed them into a sunny drawing-room. They all sat down and the tall woman, who was Mrs Madden, the housekeeper, began to chat to Mrs Halligan.

'Is she strong and willing to work?' Peggy blushed. 'She seems a good type of girl, but has she any kitchen experience?'

Half-afraid, Peggy began to tell the housekeeper about Castletaggart and the shop in Market Lane, and about helping Eily and the aunts.

The woman nodded and then turned to Mrs Halligan and began to discuss conditions and pay, an hour to attend Sunday Mass and time off. Peggy listened attentively to what they were saying. Then the mistress of the house came in. Mrs Madden introduced them to Mrs Elizabeth Rowan.

'Well, Mrs Madden, have we got ourselves a new kitchen maid?' enquired Mrs Rowan.

Peggy blazed red from toes to ears.

The housekeeper nodded her head. 'Yes.'

Mrs Rowan turned to talk to Peggy. She had marvellous wavy brown hair and a gentle face.

'Well, Peggy, welcome to Rushton. I hope you'll be

happy in service here.'

When Mrs Rowan smiled Peggy couldn't help but notice how small and even her teeth were, almost a perfect match for the set of pearls around her neck.

'Now, Peggy,' said Mrs Madden, 'I'll take you downstairs to meet Mrs O'Connor the cook, and Kitty, but first of all say your goodbyes to Mrs Halligan.' They all went into the hallway.

Peggy shuffled a bit. She felt awkward and strange, and didn't trust herself not to get upset.

'Now, Peggy, don't let me down. This time things will be fine.'

Peggy nodded, struck dumb. She wanted to thank Mags Halligan, but she couldn't get the words out. She stood looking up at the staircase as the women walked to the door and said farewell to each other.

'Good luck, Peggy,' called Mrs Halligan, as she turned and waved goodbye from the steps.

The hallway was dark and cluttered with hat stands and all kinds of bric-a-brac. Standing there Peggy could see right up through the three upper stories of the house, to some kind of glass square which was hidden in the roof. The sun pushed its way through this, creating a pattern on the tiled floor. Peggy followed Mrs Madden down the stairs to the kitchen.

She pushed in a green-painted door. Although it was a bright sunny day outside, very little sunlight managed to creep in through the kitchen's small narrow windows.

'This is young Peggy O'Driscoll, our new kitchen maid,' announced Mrs Madden.

The cook turned around.

'Welcome, my dear, I'm Mrs O'Connor. I'm the cook

and head of the kitchen. I'll be the one who'll train you in and show you what's what. Kitty, will you come here a minute and leave what you're at.'

A girl who looked a little older than Peggy was peeling a large basin of potatoes. She wiped her hands and sauntered over.

'Now, Kitty, will you show this lassie where your room is, as I'm too busy to be traipsing up to the top of the house. My feet are killing me anyway with this heat.'

Nodding, Kitty turned and led the way through another green-painted door, across patterned tiles and up narrow wooden stairs. It was a steep four flights up and the other girl never once looked back or stopped to offer Peggy a hand. By the time they reached the bedroom, Peggy was out of breath and panting. The room was small but clean, with two narrow beds.

'That's mine,' stated Kitty, pointing to the bed nearer the window. 'Yours is the other one.'

'That's fine,' agreed Peggy, touching the brass rail and feeling the cover. It was multicoloured, as if lots of odds and ends of material had been stitched and joined like bunches of autumn leaves gathered together. It looked old and well washed, but Peggy thought it was beautiful.

'That's American quilting,' Kitty informed her. 'Here, put your things in the bottom two drawers and there's hooks on the wall for hanging things. Come on, we'd better get back down or Mrs O'Connor will eat us and there's mounds to do before dinner time.'

Back in the kitchen Kitty disappeared into the scullery. Mrs O'Connor was busy cutting meat into thin slices.

'Here, girl, roll up your sleeves and give a hand with finishing the potatoes. Then you can get a start on preparing fruit for a summer tart.'

Peggy stood there. No one had chatted to her or asked her where she came from. A flash of Eily working in the kitchen back home in Market Lane stabbed like a knife. She bit her lip and decided to concentrate on her work. In no time all the potatoes were peeled and shone palely in the bowl. Mrs O'Connor then plonked a large basket of strawberries, raspberries and plums down in front of her.

'Now, sort through that lot – and no picking, my girl.'

Peggy could feel tears well up in her eyes but she didn't give in to them. She could hear Kitty banging pots and pans and singing to herself in the scullery. Mrs O'Connor was moving over and back between a large range and the pantry. Every so often she would go to the kitchen door and pull it backwards and forwards to send a breath of fresh air into the kitchen. It was a hot clammy day. At times Peggy caught a glimpse of the housekeeper outside in the garden.

About half an hour later, Peggy realised with a start that the cook was standing in front of her.

'Now, girl, here's a glass of my own lemonade to cool you down.'

A large jug filled with ice and water and lemons stood on the table. Peggy took a sip from her glass. It was sharp and bitter, yet just what she needed.

Mrs O'Connor winked at her as she took a long gulp from her own glass. 'Got to look after my own! We'll have that dinner on in no time and when all the hubbub has died down we'll have a chat. Tell Kitty to come in here and get a drink too.'

Peggy fetched Kitty.

'If there's one thing I hate, it's pots! They'll be the death of me,' groaned Kitty.

There were just finishing off the lemonade when Mrs Madden appeared in the doorway, her arms laden with flowers. They were tumbling all over the place. Peggy ran to help her. She had never touched such blooms.

'Well, Mrs O'Connor, how I envy you the time to relax and have a cool drink in the midst of preparations for dinner guests,' said the woman as she made her way to a small area with a large white sink surrounded by shelves of jugs, vases and containers of every size and shape.

'That old rip!' muttered Mrs O'Connor under her breath, her face purple with annoyance as she motioned to Kitty to get back to work.

The housekeeper produced a sharp scissors and began to trim and cut the flowers and arrange them deftly. She then curtly announced to Kitty where they were to be put.

'Drawing-room, Kitty.'

'Main hallway.'

'Bottom of the stairs.'

'Landing.'

'Dining-room, girl.'

Peggy felt like laughing as Kitty slopped water along the tiled floors and rushed up and down the stairs. She pulled a face at Kitty.

'You, girl, stop making silly faces and get a mop and dry up that floor,' ordered the housekeeper before going upstairs with the last floral arrangement.

It was long after dark when Peggy stopped work. Her shoulders and arms and the backs of her legs ached. Earlier she had felt her eyes shutting while Mrs O'Connor was telling her something. At seven o'clock she had managed to eat quickly a few slices of meat, some thick crusty bread and a piece of rather stale sponge cake. At eleven o'clock she trudged up the stairs at last. She just about managed to hang her dress on the hook before stretching out on the bed. The room was warm and she let the bedclothes cover just the lower half of her body. She wanted to stay awake and chat to Kitty and find out about the place, but exhaustion won the battle against curiosity.

CHAPTER 14

The Likes of Us

'PEGGY, PEGGY, GET UP QUICK. Mrs O'Connor will kill you if you don't make a start.'

It was dawn. Bleary eyed, Peggy tried to remember where she was. She threw some water from the white wash-bowl between the beds on to her face before dragging on her dress. Kitty passed her the hairbrush and helped her to tidy her hair.

'We'll talk later,' assured the other girl, pushing Peggy out the door, as she turned to fix her own hair.

The kitchen felt cool and the smell of last night's dinner still hung in the air. The range needed emptying and the coals had to be topped up. Peggy began to fill the large kettle. Mrs O'Connor ambled in, her face pale in the early morning light. She told Peggy to fetch bacon and eggs and a bowl. In no time breakfast was cooked and ready to serve. Peggy watched with amazement as Kitty lifted the heavy tray up the stairs, but she seemed surefooted and well able to manage.

Once her own breakfast was over, Peggy was curious to discover more about the Rowans.

'How many are there in the family?' she asked Kitty.

'Well,' began Kitty, 'there's the Mistress, Mrs

Elizabeth – you've met her. Then the Master, Mr Gregory Rowan – he's some kind of banker. Miss Roxanne is fifteen and a right little minx. Watch out for her. She may look as if butter wouldn't melt in her mouth but ...'

'Kitty!' warned the cook.

'Anyways, then there's Simon, he's a pet. He's six years old. There's always cousins or uncles or aunts staying too, but it's just themselves at the moment.'

Just then Mrs Madden appeared at the table.

'Kitty, I've warned you about gossiping! Now, get back upstairs, there's plenty of cleaning to be done this morning, and Peggy, when you've finished the washing up I want to see you in my office.'

Peggy filled the sink with boiling hot water and began to scrub and scrub, plunging her hands into the greasy water. I'd better get used to this! she thought.

An hour later she made her way to the housekeeper's small room. A walnut desk was covered in papers and a few ledgers lay open. Mrs Madden had two or three outfits over her arm.

'Now, try these on and we'll see what fits you.'

The first was way too small, and Peggy noticed that it smelled faintly of stale sweat. Mrs Madden tossed it over the chair. The minute Peggy pulled on the second one she knew it was just right. The material was light green cotton with a tiny pattern of dainty leaves in plum colour which gave the appearance of stripes. It had long sleeves, with extra-long buttoned cuffs so that the sleeves could be rolled up for work. Peggy twirled around in it.

'It's just beautiful and perfect,' she smiled.

The housekeeper then produced a dark slate grey

dress, made to the same pattern. Peggy felt it made her look drab and dreary.

'Yes, that will do nicely,' nodded the woman.

She then gave Peggy three white aprons and matching white cuff protectors, and a neat white collar and two caps.

'Keep one apron and the collar for good wear. Also, I expect you to keep a civil tongue in your head and keep yourself clean and tidy. I won't stand for a slovenly appearance. Now, do we understand each other? There'll be a warmer uniform, much the same, for when the cold weather comes. Any stitching or mending needed, you attend to it yourself.'

'Yes, Mrs Madden.'

'Work hard, my girl, and I'll be pleased with you. I'm a fair woman and only too pleased to help a girl like yourself fresh from Ireland. It's how I started myself.'

Peggy looked at her, but obviously Mrs Madden was not prepared to tell her any more.

'Now run along upstairs and put on the green and tie up your hair, and then get straight down again to attend to your duties.'

Peggy had just come back down to the kitchen when she noticed the lady of the house standing there discussing the week's menu with the cook. Elizabeth Rowan was the prettiest woman Peggy had ever seen in her life. Her skin was clear, without a blemish or freckle. Peggy wrinkled her nose thinking of the bridge of freckles that no amount of scrubbing would remove. Such fashion and style the Mistress had – a beautiful lace-ruffled blouse and a skirt, the colour of the soft moss back home, that fell in flounces almost to the floor.

'Little Peggy, isn't it?'

Peggy almost dropped to the floor and with the brush and pan still in her hands went towards the sweet voice and accent.

'Yes, Ma'am,' she said, and blushed.

'Well, I hope you've settled in. Mrs Madden has fitted you out already, I'm glad to see. I hope you won't let myself or Mrs Halligan down.'

'No, Ma'am,' promised Peggy.

'Mrs O'Connor will tell you what needs to be done. She runs the kitchen like an army regiment, spick and span, good food, on time and everything in its place. I leave it all in her good hands.' The Mistress threw a glance of relief at Mrs O'Connor. The cook reminded Peggy of a large wood pigeon, almost cooing with pride as the other woman went back upstairs.

'She's a good kind mistress, Peggy, remember that. There isn't a bad bone in her and I should know. I've worked for her ever since my poor husband Paddy was taken nine years ago. My daughter worked here too, but she's married with babies herself now. Would you ever believe I'm a grandmother, Peggy? Mrs Rowan is a fine woman, mind you, even if she can't boil an egg or make a cup of tea for herself. Not everyone can live their life in the kitchen. That's for the likes of us!'

Peggy nodded. She felt as if a stone had sunk in the waters of her spirit at the words 'the likes of us'. She looked at Mrs O'Connor whose face was round and full of kindness. Years of standing over saucepans and pots seemed to have boiled her skin a lusty pink.

'Now, lassie, sit down and listen well to me and I'll

tell you what's expected of you,' Mrs O'Connor began.
'A good kitchen maid ...'

* * *

Peggy sat on the bed, her knees pulled up under her
chin. Her head was reeling and she had a headache. She
would never remember half of what Mrs O'Connor told
her. There was just too much for one person to do, let
alone remember. She had nearly laughed in the middle
of the long list thinking the cook was playing a joke on
her, but one look at the serious face was enough to tell
her the woman was in earnest.

This was meant to be the mid-afternoon rest period.

'I always insist on an hour's rest every afternoon,'
Mrs O'Connor had told her. 'It's the one thing that Mrs
Madden and I are in total agreement about – an hour or
more to sleep, relax and rest your feet, or get a breath of
fresh air. 'Tis the least a body could expect.'

Peggy was all wound up, her brain bursting with all
the new information. How could she possibly relax
when she felt like this?

'Well, Peggy, aren't you having a nap in this heat?'
Kitty pulled the door open to let some air circulate between it and the window in the small room.

Kitty had stripped off her uniform. She lay across the
narrow bed, dressed just in her underclothing, her arms
and legs spreadeagled trying to cool down. Peggy
couldn't resist the temptation. She put her hand in the
full water jug on the stand between the beds and flicked
the water all over Kitty.

'I'm drowned, God almighty!' shouted Kitty. She shot
up in the bed and grabbed the jug, and for an instant

Peggy thought she was going to empty the jug of water over her. Instead Kitty placed the large wash-bowl on the floor and poured all the water from the jug into it. Then she gingerly put one foot into the bowl. 'God, that's gorgeous.'

Peggy was over in a flash, standing on one foot with the other thrust into the blissfully cold water. Soon the throbbing in her foot and her tiredness was easing away.

'Aren't we the right pair, paddling in a wash-bowl instead of a cool mountain stream or the waves at the seaside?'

They pulled the bowl along the floor, then both of them sat on the side of Kitty's bed and dangled their feet in the water.

'Peggy, I'm glad you've come. 'Twas awful lonely here the last month or so since Norah Owens left.'

'Where did she go?' enquired Peggy, curious about the fate of the previous occupant of her bed and uniform.

'Out west,' announced Kitty, 'across prairies and plains. There's twice the money to be made in places like California. Norah's wild – she says it's a land of opportunity. She tried to talk me into going with her, but I told her I know what side my bread is buttered on!'

Peggy nodded sagely and stifled a pang of regret that she had not had the chance to meet the wild Norah Owens. Still, it was nice to have Kitty.

Over the next few days Kitty and Peggy began to lay the stones of a strong friendship. Often at night they chatted, taking it in turn to tell their stories until they heard the snore from the opposite bed.

Kitty's family had left Ireland in 1847, when the Great

Famine was at its worst. Kitty was ten then. The voyage was a nightmare and after a month at sea almost half of the passengers died of cabin fever, including Kitty's mother and father and two brothers. At journey's end all that was left of the Murphy family was Kitty and her four-year-old sister, May. They were placed in an orphanage. The following year Kitty started work.

Her first position was as a scullery maid in a house in the centre of Boston. They gave her a uniform, a bed in the room beside the scullery, and they fed her. Other than that she was not paid one cent for the whole year. Eventually she ran away and went back to the orphanage. Her little sister had been moved to another home and she could not trace her. Next she worked for an old lady who was a recluse and lived miles from her nearest neighbour. Provisions were delivered once a week and in emergencies Kitty would walk miles to the nearest store. But the rest of the week was spent cooking and cleaning almost in total solitude. The old lady cut herself off from Kitty too by reading and writing letters all day. Kitty dared not run away again. And then finally Mrs Bridgeton died and the solicitors had helped to get her this position here with the Rowan family in Greenbay.

'This is as good as you'll get, Peggy. I know that and anyways hard work never killed anybody,' declared Kitty.

Kitty might be a few years older than Peggy, but she had missed out on so much in life. Peggy decided she would do her best to make it up to her. For her part, Kitty had made up her mind to help Peggy settle in and buckle down to work, and to make the most of her new life in Boston.

Across the bare floorboards they held hands as they drifted to sleep in the summer heat of the attic room.

* * *

The week's routine was strict and rigid, but at least everyone knew exactly what they had to do and there were few misunderstandings. One day blended into another. At night, Peggy's bones and muscles ached. Kitty would hold her legs and rub them, and Peggy moaned, feeling that her veins would burst with cramps.

'Don't make too much noise, Peggy,' urged Kitty, 'or we'll have Mrs Madden up complaining to us.' The housekeeper slept in the room below them.

There wasn't a day or night that Peggy didn't feel homesick and lonely. She wrote a long letter to Nano and Eily, and day after day she waited for their reply.

Often in the evenings the cook and the two maids would sit in the kitchen and wait for the bells to ring. Mrs O'Connor always managed to save for herself Mr Rowan's copy of the paper from the day before. She would pull her heavy chair up near the warmth of the range and read out snippets of news. Her favourites were the murders and missing children stories, which she read with zeal, checking every few minutes that Peggy and Kitty were still listening.

It didn't take long for Peggy to discover that Kitty could not read or write. She loved to listen to Mrs O'Connor and was thrilled when Peggy read the latest serial story from the newspaper for her in bed at night.

'Wouldn't you like to be able to read a bit yourself, Kitty?' asked Peggy. 'Didn't anyone ever teach you?'

Kitty looked ashamed, but shook her head.

'I don't remember. Maybe once in the orphans' home, but mostly there was the other stuff to do – sewing, cleaning, helping with the little ones and the babies. I'd better things to do with myself,' protested the older girl.

'I could teach you a bit, if you wanted,' offered Peggy.

'No, I don't think so – it would only cause trouble,' muttered Kitty, trying to avoid Peggy's eyes.

'Trouble? What kind of trouble? Do you mean the trouble I'd take teaching you at night?'

'No, no – it just might get us into trouble. Anyways, it's not worth it. It doesn't matter that much what I can or can't do.'

Peggy turned on her, furious. 'Matter? Of course it matters! Do you want to stay a stupid skivvy for the rest of your days?'

A tense silence hung in the air. Peggy could feel the blood pulsing in her ears. Maybe she'd gone too far, said too much. Kitty looked straight at her.

'No,' she whispered.

'Well!' Peggy felt like cheering, but instead she just smiled. Then she began to wonder how exactly you'd go about teaching all about the alphabet and the words and sounds.

Still, if Kitty was willing to try, then so was she.

'Peggy, could you teach me to write my own name? I'd like that.'

'That'll be the first lesson,' promised Peggy.

By the next night the attic room was full of scraps of paper with KITTY MURPHY scrawled across them in large uneven letters.

CHAPTER 15

Roxanne

 THE ROWAN FAMILY USUALLY kept their distance and had little to do with the maids, except for young Simon who loved to be in and out of the kitchen. He would stand up on a chair watching Mrs O'Connor and she would let him lick bowls and give her mixtures a stir sometimes, for luck. He often ran in from the garden demanding a jar or tin to put some unfortunate creature in and would arrive back to show them all kinds of insects, the like of which Peggy had never seen before. The American insects seemed a lot bigger than the Irish ones, she thought. 'Maybe they're better fed,' laughed Kitty.

Roxanne, the only daughter, was fifteen and as flawlessly beautiful as her mother. She had almost silver-blonde hair which she wore in ringlets around her face, showing off her large blue eyes to advantage. She played the piano every day and studied with a tutor who came to instruct her in French and English, literature and art. Sometimes other young ladies would call and Peggy would watch from the kitchen step as they went for a short drive around Greenbay by carriage. They were always chaperoned by one of the mothers.

Roxanne rarely came down the stairs to the kitchen area and if she did it was usually to complain. One Saturday she arrived at the kitchen door and called Mrs Madden. Kitty and the housekeeper had immediately to begin to re-press Roxanne's pale peach dress as she wanted it for dinner.

Peggy was set to restitching the hem of Roxanne's favourite petticoat which had snagged when she was out shopping that morning.

'I'm no good at sewing and mending,' Peggy had admitted from the start, but she had been met with polite disbelief by the rest of the household.

She kept sticking the needle in her finger as she tried to copy the fine stitches of her predecessor. She even managed to stitch the petticoat to her apron at one stage, she was in such a mood trying to sew.

An hour later, Roxanne stormed downstairs and flung the petticoat at her.

'It's got specks of blood on it – her blood,' she screamed, pointing at Peggy. 'I will not wear it till it's been laundered.'

Peggy had never felt so embarrassed.

'There, Miss Roxanne, I am afraid you will have to wait until Monday when the washerwomen come around,' Mrs Madden replied firmly.

The daughter of the house flounced off back upstairs muttering comments about 'those Irish!'

* * *

A few days later Peggy heard excited voices of family

and friends who had come to wish Miss Roxanne a happy sixteenth birthday and toast her good health. Mrs O'Connor had provided an extravagant supper and a special cake.

Looking at the cake on the silver tray, Peggy remembered the beautiful cakes and confections that Auntie Nano and Lena used to make – and she longed again for the kitchen of Market Lane.

'Peggy, Mrs O'Connor, look!' Young Simon was standing at the kitchen door with a little puppy squirming in his arms. 'He's the best present I ever saw. Isn't Roxanne lucky? Aunt Melissa gave him to her.'

'He's an angel. Look, Peggy, isn't he lovely?' joked Mrs O'Connor.

A shiver of fear passed through Peggy the minute she saw the dog. With a burst of energy he bounced out of young Simon's arms and began to scamper around the kitchen, exploring every nook and cranny.

Peggy stepped back near the scullery. She tried to control the shakes that were tingling through her. Years ago, when she was only seven, a pack of dogs, wild and starving, had attacked her, and since then she had never lost her fear of dogs no matter what they were like. She just couldn't stand them being near her. The puppy stood panting with excitement, his tail wagging and his long tongue out, staring at her, almost touching her feet.

'Go away! Get lost!' she muttered.

'Bonaparte! Good dog!' Roxanne, looking more gorgeous than ever, suddenly appeared in the kitchen. She came to a halt right in front of Peggy.

'Isn't he a beautiful dog?' announced Roxanne.

Peggy was so scared of the little creature, she could barely stutter, 'He's grand, Miss.'

Roxanne bent down and scooped him up.

'Come and pet him, then.' The older girl stared at Peggy.

She knows, thought Peggy – she can read my mind! Peggy tried to put out her hand and force herself to touch the shiny brown and white coat. She just couldn't do it.

'Are you scared of a little bit of a thing like Bonaparte?' jeered Roxanne.

Peggy felt like pulling the other girl's curls as she looked into the smug face.

'No, it's not that, Miss, it's just that my hands are greasy from the pots,' she announced, inspired.

Bored at last, Roxanne turned her attention to the others.

Peggy stood rigid and still until both the dog and his mistress had gone back upstairs. Only then, to everyone's surprise, did the tears seep out of her. She tried to explain her fear but nobody listened. There and then she decided to keep well out of the way of the dog, who was given the run of the house. But five days later trouble struck.

* * *

Peggy had just finished cleaning out the grate and resetting the fire in Roxanne's room. I'll light it later, she thought. The sun streamed in, showing the bright feminine room to full advantage, with its drapes and frills and cherrywood wardrobe and dressing table.

Peggy moved down the hallway and was just starting to clean the Master's room when she heard the screams.

Roxanne appeared in her dressing gown. 'Mother, come and see what she's done!'

Peggy looked up. 'What is it, Miss Roxanne?' Perhaps she'd dropped some ash on the mat or maybe the fuel had fallen out. She went back to the room to check.

'Mother, look at my dress!' cried Roxanne.'I need it for my tea party with the Abbots this afternoon. Can't you see what she's done?'

Peggy looked at the dress. It had been flung rather carelessly across the bed. It was pale cream, with a neat waist and butter-coloured panels. Right across the centre lay a succession of black smudges and marks.

'Ashes and dust all over my dress. Why couldn't that stupid maid, Bridget or whatever she's called, keep her filthy hands to herself.'

'I didn't touch the dress, Miss Roxanne, I give you my word,' Peggy answered, totally flabbergasted by Roxanne's reaction. Peggy moved closer to look at the dress and then she noticed it – there was a definite pattern to the marks.

'Miss Roxanne, those are not finger marks. If you look closely you'll see they're paw marks. Bonaparte must have come in from the garden. Every day I clean up marks just like them from the floor and paintwork.'

The Mistress nodded at Peggy. 'Now, Roxanne, you

know Peggy is right. Anyway I've told you to keep the dog out of your room.'

The two girls stared at each other and Peggy realised that she had made a dangerous enemy.

CHAPTER 16

The Wild Flowers

'GIRLS, THIS HEAT'LL BE THE DEATH OF US ALL,' groaned Mrs O'Connor. The kitchen was stifling. Peggy's cheeks were bright red from running around and her uniform stuck to her.

'The minute this lunch is over, lassies, the two of you are to run off and get a bit of fresh air. 'Tis too hot to be sitting in the attic,' advised the cook.

Kitty waited impatiently for Peggy to finish her work.

'This is the last thing to put away, I swear,' said Peggy, closing the scullery door.

They walked down by the small kitchen garden and out the back gate.

'Which way will we go?' asked Peggy.

'Follow me!'

Passing other newer houses and a small laneway flanked by hedgerows, they were suddenly looking out over field after field of grass and corn.

'Oh, Kitty, it's just like home!' gasped Peggy.

'I don't remember that very well,' shrugged Kitty.

They climbed over a neat wooden fence into a wide open meadow. The long grass almost reached to their hips. They threw themselves down on its soft carpet and stretched out on the cushion of green beneath them.

'One shoe, two shoe,' laughed Peggy, kicking her shoes off and up in the air. A feeling of pure pleasure ran through her as her feet felt the once familiar sensation of grass and soil. She wriggled her toes.

Kitty had hitched up her skirt to her knees and rolled back her cuffs and sleeves. Her skin was pale and her mouse-brown hair was dull, but her face was soft and gentle.

'Look at that sky!' Peggy stared at its vivid blueness. 'Not a cloud in sight.' She squinted against the sun. A cricket chirped its strange cry, such a foreign sound.

She closed her eyes. She was back home and Eily and herself were lying in the fields outside Castletaggart. Autumn was in the air. Soon there would be blackberries. Every bush was heavy with blossom or fruit. They'd come back and pick them when they were ripe ...

'Peggy! Peggy!'

She blinked her eyes. Kitty was tapping her shoulder.

'Wake up! I think you're getting sunburnt. You dozed off.'

Peggy sat up. 'I was dreaming of home.' She felt strangely confused and empty. She wondered if anyone back in Ireland ever thought of her anymore. She told Kitty about her dream.

'Will I tell you a secret, Peggy? I have only one

dream,' confided Kitty. 'I dream I'm walking along, sometimes in the town, sometimes in the countryside, and I see this girl and she looks just like me – she's smaller and younger and prettier, but I know her and she knows me. It's my sister, May ... Do you suppose dreams ever come true, Peggy?'

Peggy nodded dumbly, not trusting herself to speak. Both of them here in a field in the middle of nowhere and thinking about their sisters ...

Finally they got to their feet, stretched lazily, then wandered around to gather wild flowers. The field was covered in them, as were all the fields nearby. Swathes of flowers – vivid blue cornflowers, spikes of pink rose-bay, moondaisies, white frothy yarrow, bluebonnets – blazed with colour in the sunlight. Wind and rain, animals and even man might flatten them or knock them down, but they would still spring back again and dance and bow in the summer breeze and sun. Their untamed beauty helped to banish any sadness the girls felt.

'Come on, we'd best head home,' said Kitty, brushing grass seed and pollen off the back of Peggy's hair.

They carried home bunches of the simple flowers and for the rest of those long hot summer weeks they kept filling and re-filling two jam jars to brighten their attic room.

CHAPTER 17

The Kitchen Sink

'KITTY, TELL ME HONESTLY, DO I stink?' Peggy looked at her friend for reassurance.

'We all pong, a bit anyways, working in this heat,' answered Kitty diplomatically.

'You're not telling me straight, Kitty.'

'Look, we do our best. We only have a jug and basin to wash in. There's a tin bath out near the woodshed – I used it a few times up here in the room, but you have to lug it up the stairs and then carry up hot water to fill it.'

'All the way up here!' At once Peggy realised this involved far too much heavy work.

The Rowans had a family bathroom where there was a large white bath. In the mornings the room was always steamy and the smell of perfume and soap lingered in the air.

The next day Peggy got up the courage to go to Mrs Madden's room. The woman looked up.

'Yes, Peggy, what is it?'

'I wanted to ask about bathing myself.'

The housekeeper looked at her questioningly. She said nothing.

'I mean – am I let use the bathroom?'

Mrs Madden stood up and Peggy could spot a vein throbbing in her neck. 'Under no circumstances, Peggy. You will not dare to wash yourself there. It's up to you to make your own washing and hygiene arrangements, whatever they may be.'

Peggy left the room, shamefaced. She went out to the woodshed and in the storage room beside it she rooted and discovered an old perambulator, two broken chairs, a dented enamel bucket and finally the tin bath. It was rusty and the suspicion of a hole lurked near the middle in the bottom of it. She could guess the lecture she would get if the water dripped from the bath and through the ceiling to the housekeeper's room. It's not fair, she thought. We're expected to be clean and neat and yet we're not given the chance! As she came back into the kitchen she passed the large sink near the door. It wasn't used much. Would it be possible ... ?

The next day the house was quiet. The Mistress and Miss Roxanne had gone to get new dresses fitted. Mrs O'Connor was having tea with a widow friend of hers who was a cook in a house at the other end of Greenbay. She had put on a large white bonnet and then disappeared. Kitty had strict instructions for a simple meal to be served, as the Master and Mistress were dining out that night and Mrs Madden was working in her office upstairs.

'This is just the time,' thought Peggy. She put on two giant pots of water to boil and charged all the way up the stairs to her room. Kitty was breathing heavily in a deep sleep. Peggy got her spare clothes and underthings, and her large wash-towel. From the wash-stand, she grabbed a bar of lemon-scented soap that Mrs Madden had given Kitty, and raced back down the stairs. She placed the big black stopper in the sink. She pulled up a chair, then lugged the pots of boiling water over. It was almost half-full. She added some cold water as she didn't want to be roasted alive. She tested it – it was just perfect. She closed the back door and got out of her uniform. The whole house was still and quiet – all you could hear was the tick of the kitchen clock. In a minute she was naked.

Oh no! I'll need a jug for my hair, she thought. Luckily there was a big enamel one under the sink. She got up on the chair and gently stepped into the back-kitchen sink. The water was warm and welcoming. The sink was too short to lie down in, but at least she could sit fairly comfortably and almost stretch her legs. She turned around and got on to her knees, then lowered her head and scalp into the water and soaped her hair with the lemon soap. She dipped it back into the water to get the lather off, then poured the jug of spare water over her head and shoulders. Now she could relax. She let the warm water soak into her. It was bliss. The skin on her feet felt rough and hard and her hands and elbows needed a bit of attention too. She gently massaged the soap around her neck and back. At home Eily and herself used to wash each other's backs on bath night in Market Lane. Washing your troubles and cares away – that's what her old Aunt Nano would have said.

Then as if in a nightmare, Peggy heard a step. Good God! Who was it? Mrs Madden? – she'd be killed! The Mistress? – it didn't bear thinking about. Peggy lay paralysed in the water. Should she jump out and wrap herself in the towel? – but then they'd hear her. Maybe if she stayed perfectly still whoever it was would go away.

But the door burst open and little Simon Rowan stood in front of her. Peggy felt every cell in her body turn puce. The little boy looked at her and didn't bat an eyelid, as if naked young girls around the house was an everyday occurrence. His big blue eyes and innocent face turned towards her. His skin had a healthy glow and his usually neat fair hair was all askew.

'Quick, Peggy! There's a strange creature under the gooseberry bushes. I'll need a cage – well, a jar anyway – to catch it. I had it cornered.'

Peggy could have hugged him. Instead she just said, 'Master Simon, run out and guard it and I'll get the strongest container you ever saw and will be out to you in a minute – otherwise it might escape.'

In a flash, Simon disappeared out the back door and Peggy was standing dripping all over the tiled floor.

Never in her whole life did Peggy get dressed so quickly. Briskly she rubbed her skin dry and pulled on her fresh underthings and then put on the grey dress and a fresh apron. She tried to smooth down her hair, then dried the ends of it with the rough towel and slipped on her shoes. She emptied the sink and put the chair back. The dirty clothes and towel she rolled in a bundle and stuffed into the closet under the sink and then, grabbing an empty biscuit tin from the pantry, she chased out to where young Simon lay sprawled on the dirt.

'Peggy, you've been ages, what kept you?'

She chuckled to herself.

'Look, Master Simon, will this do? Mrs O'Connor

usually stores brandy snaps in it.'

He grabbed the circular biscuit tin and motioned to Peggy to crouch down. He pointed eagerly towards a clump of scutch grass growing between the gooseberry bushes.

'Look,' whispered Simon.

Two tiny little eyes stared back at her. It was a very small baby field mouse, which must have got separated from its mother. It was trapped and scared and Peggy knew exactly how it felt.

'Hold the lid, Peggy, and get down beside me.'

Simon was reaching out, trying to force the mouse to run into the tin.

Peggy managed half by accident and half on purpose to close the lid just before the mouse ran into it. Simon tried to throw himself on the tiny animal, but Peggy spotted it darting aside and weaving in and out of the gooseberry bushes before it disappeared. Simon groaned in frustration and then sat up.

Peggy laughed. Both she and the mouse had had a narrow escape.

CHAPTER 18

The Day Off

FRIDAY! FRIDAY! PEGGY WAS SO excited she thought she would burst. At last her month's trial was up.

Her first wages and afternoon off, and both on the one day – it was too good to be true. She had planned exactly where she was going.

Mrs Madden called Peggy to her room.

'Sit down, Peggy. Are you happy here?' Peggy nodded. 'Mrs O'Connor and I are both well pleased with your work. I have your wages here. There's no deduction for uniforms as in some households, and Mrs O'Connor told me there were no breakages, so it's the full amount.'

She passed Peggy a sealed brown envelope. As Peggy got up to leave, Mrs Madden added: 'I know it's exciting and tempting when you get your first wages, but may I suggest you save most of it and spend only on essentials. Boston winters are cold and hard and you will most likely need a warm coat later on and strong boots for outside. Kitty will tell you where to go for such things.'

Peggy tried to look sensible and calm as she closed the door behind her. She tore open the envelope. Disappointment washed over her. This couldn't be right!

There were at least two dollars missing. The house-keeper must have made a mistake. She rapped on the door and marched back in. The housekeeper looked up in surprise.

'Yes, my girl, what is it?'

'It's not right, Mrs Madden, there's some money missing. You must have added it wrong.'

'Added it wrong! How dare you, you little chit.' The housekeeper lifted up her ledger and opened it at the day's date.

Peggy spread the money on the desk.

'No, Peggy, that's all correct. Don't forget – part of your first quarter year's salary goes to Mrs Halligan as her fee.' Peggy stared at her. 'Did you forget, child?' she asked.

Peggy didn't answer. She felt a fool for kicking up such a fuss. She managed to mumble an apology and escape. All the rest of the morning she fumed. Mrs Halligan – how are you! At two-thirty Mrs O'Connor told her to tidy herself and enjoy her afternoon off.

Peggy walked along Greenbay Avenue, hoping to get a lift. After about fifteen minutes a horse and small carriage stopped beside her. She recognised the uniform. It was the coachman from the house next door.

'Hop in, my dear, I presume you're city bound?'

'Yes,' she smiled.

As they flew along the roadway, his cape flapping in the breeze, he told her about the people who lived in the houses they passed. They slowed down as they got to the city centre. He had a long list of jobs to do, and he would be leaving again at six o'clock. If she was ready and waiting he would give her a lift back.

'Now, I'll not delay, so you'll have a long walk home otherwise,' he warned in his American drawl, still strange to Peggy's ears.

Peggy was delighted and thanked him.

She loved Boston city. The streets were clean and wide and tree-lined. The buildings stood in neat rows, the houses had curved fronts and bow windows – and always in the distance was the beautiful harbour. Kitty had told her about the huge public common and the broad, fast-flowing Charles River. There was so much to see that Peggy didn't know where to start. She looked in the sparkling glass windows of a busy store where the whole display was given over to fashion. There were bonnets and matching muffs and two beautiful velvet dresses. In the lower part of the window, gloves and small evening bags and bottles of French scent were displayed.

Fine ladies wearing fashionable bonnets and smelling of heady perfumes passed by her and disappeared inside the brass-edged doors.

If I buy anything there I'll be skint, but it won't stop me looking, she decided. She walked all around the fashionable part of town and then meandered down to where the streets became narrow, winding and cluttered. Here she came across a large general store. A cheery bell rang as each customer made their entry. A middle-aged woman directed Peggy to the clothing area. There was rail after rail of dresses and neat piles of folded blouses and aprons. A long drawer-unit held displays of stockings and warm vests and such things. Peggy looked over the rail of coats. They were mostly black or dark green or a deep burgundy. They felt and looked warm. She shuddered when she saw the price tag and decided to purchase a warm pair of woollen stockings instead. Then she was lured into buying a small jar of honeysuckle-scented handcream, which promised to 'banish dry chafed skin'. That was enough for one day.

Back outside she asked a red-faced man for directions and started to walk briskly towards Number 49, Empire Hill. As she climbed up the hill she passed a corner building. The windows were covered in portraits of women, men and children. They were not paintings, and they looked so real! They were sepia-coloured mostly, though some had been tinted with colours. There was a notice on the window: 'The perfect gift to send home – a treasure for loved ones to keep. One sitting and a guaranteed print. Walk inside to our daguerreotype studio.'

Peggy looked at the pictures and noted the address for another time. Today she had other fish to fry. Quickly She traced her way to Number 49 and rang the bell. Nancy opened the door.

'Hello, Nancy. I'm looking for Sarah. Is she still here? I'm sorry I haven't time to chat,' said Peggy breathlessly.

Nancy shook her head. 'Sarah Connolly left about ten days ago. She's lodging with her brothers in rooms at the back of Russell Street and is still working in Goldman's shirt factory.'

'I've missed her, then. I have to get a lift back at six o'clock.' Peggy was very disappointed.

'Well, wait now – you can run down the street and catch her as she gets out of Goldman's. She should be finishing her shift in a few minutes.'

Promising to visit again when she had the chance, Peggy took to her heels, wrapping her shawl tightly around her. She was back down the hill and across the two streets in no time, then she saw the tall ugly building that she knew was Goldman's.

After ten minutes' waiting she was rewarded by a glimpse of Sarah Connolly stepping through the heavy rust-coloured doors. Sarah spotted Peggy and ran straight to her.

'Oh, Peggy, I've missed you,' she said.

'Sarah, I've so much to tell you. But how are things going for you?'

'We have rooms two blocks away and I've been put to doing button work at Goldman's.'

They were both so delighted to see each other that they could hardly stop talking and neither could get a word in edgeways. Peggy held on to Sarah's arm as they walked through Russell Street towards the large ramshackle building and up to the third floor where Sarah's new home was.

They had two bedrooms and a small living and cooking area. A row of shirts and long-johns hung from a rope across the long window. Straight away Sarah began to refuel the simple stove and then lifted a pot of thick soup on to cook. Peggy realised her friend was all done in. Her face was pale, with deep purple shadows under her eyes, her hands were zigzagged with cuts and looked sore and stiff. The nails were broken and chipped, and blackened and darkened from the button work. After a hard day's work at the factory which started at seven o'clock in the morning, Sarah then had to turn around and cook and clean for herself and her two brothers, John and James.

'When the boys get better jobs and have learnt a bit about the building trade we'll be able to afford a nicer place,' Sarah assured Peggy.

Peggy refused anything to eat, but managed to swallow a quick cup of tea.

'I have to go, Sarah, but maybe if I get my Sunday off in a few weeks we'll see each other then.'

The other girl looked so lost and lonely that Peggy didn't know what to do. On an impulse she reached into the large pocket of her dress. She pulled out the jar of honeysuckle handcream, still in its wrapper.

'I nearly forgot, I bought you a little present.'

Tears welled up in Sarah's eyes as Peggy clambered down the stairs two at a time, and ran to get her lift. Peggy's heart felt heavy and she was silent as the horse clip-clopped its way back to Rushton.

CHAPTER 19

The Missing Ring

THE FOLLOWING WEEK PEGGY was working in the music room.

'Peggy, you're to pay special attention to washing the floor and polishing the woodwork,' Mrs Madden ordered.

'I'll get some fresh water, Mrs Madden, and do it straight away,' Peggy said.

'Apparently the dust and dirt has an effect on the piano, so make sure it's spotless.' The housekeeper went off upstairs to check Kitty's work.

The music room was beautiful. Peggy let the cloth-covered mop glide over the maplewood floor. She'd polish it up when it dried.

The piano and music stand were the centrepiece of the room. Two or three spindly chairs were placed around the walls, which were lined with crowded bookshelves. Often Peggy would stop and gaze at the inscribed leather-bound covers, longing to read what was inside.

She had to kneel and almost crawl down on the floor to reach the wood under the curved window seat. When she put in the wet cloth there certainly was plenty of dust. She was just about to squeeze out the cloth when she noticed a glint of silver. It was a ring designed in a pattern of entwined snakes. She lifted it up. She didn't like it much and shoved it in her pocket to give to Mrs Madden.

She longed to lift the lid and run her fingers on the ivory keys of the piano, but resisted the temptation. Once she finished the music room, she went back to the scullery to empty the bucket.

Kitty ran in.

'Mrs Madden wants you, Peggy, straight away in her office!'

Peggy dried her hands, ran upstairs and knocked on the housekeeper's door.

Roxanne was standing in the corner of the room, pretending to look out at the yard.

'Yes, Mrs Madden?'

'Did you just clean the music room, Peggy?'

'Yes Ma'am, I did as you asked,' she answered.

'Did you touch the piano?'

A blush of colour suffused Peggy's face. Roxanne was looking at her.

'No, Mrs Madden, I didn't touch it.' God, maybe it was broken and they were trying to blame her.

'Are you sure?'

Peggy nodded, trying to appear calm.

'She's a liar,' Roxanne declared fiercely. 'A liar and a thief.'

Suddenly it dawned on Peggy what this was all about – that old snake ring she had found in the corner under the window seat.

'I left my good ring on top of the piano when I was practising. She's stolen it.'

Peggy reached into her pocket to get the ring and put

it on the desk and explain where she found it. It was gone!

'Mrs Madden, I demand you search her. We don't want a thief at Rushton.'

'I'm sorry, Peggy. Have you anything to say?'

Peggy didn't know what to do. How could she tell the truth if she couldn't produce the ring? Then she'd be in real trouble.

Mrs Madden emptied out Peggy's apron pockets and the pockets of her uniform. She then made her open the buttons on her sleeves.

'You must be mistaken, Miss Roxanne,' the house-keeper said, trying to soothe the girl.

'Search wherever she's been and her room. She could have hidden it there!'

Kitty was called in and sent to search the scullery. Mrs O'Connor had to sit in the office with Peggy while the housekeeper searched her bedroom. Miss Roxanne followed her up to the attic stairs.

Peggy felt numb. The ring had not been on top of the piano. If it was she would not have touched it. Mrs Rowan was always leaving pairs of fine earrings all over the house – in the dining-room or the drawing-room or the bathroom. They were never touched. But the snake ring had been in the most out-of-the-way place. It could never have got there by accident.

Mrs O'Connor said nothing to Peggy.

'I didn't steal it!' pleaded Peggy.

The cook was embarrassed and fidgeted with her apron. She would not meet Peggy's eyes. Kitty came back, and stood leaning against the wall, pretending to stare out of the window. Twenty minutes later Mrs

Rowan came down to see what all the fuss was about. She stood outside the door talking to the housekeeper, the cook and Roxanne. The two maids were left on their own.

'Peggy's a thief. I know she stole it. Get rid of her, Mother,' they heard Roxanne shout.

'Kitty,' whispered Peggy. 'Kitty!'

The other girl did not turn towards her.

'You've got to help me. Please, Kitty, search and see if you can find the ring.'

Kitty refused to answer.

Peggy felt like screaming at her or even hitting her. 'I didn't steal it, I swear!' She kept her voice low. 'Kitty, we're friends – please!'

Kitty swung around. Her face had the look of a hunted animal. 'Stop it, Peggy. I don't want any trouble. I've had enough trouble already, so just leave me alone,' she hissed.

Peggy's heart sank. She realised Kitty was weak and afraid and wouldn't stand up for her. Just then the others filed back in to accuse Peggy again.

Roxanne ranted and raved.

'Thief ... Peggy is a thief ... I know she stole it. Get rid of her, Mother.'

Mrs Rowan looked flustered and upset.

'Roxanne, dear, calm down. We have no proof that Peggy took your ring. I suggest we let the matter lie and see if it turns up. Now, everyone, back to work.'

Mrs Rowan disappeared back upstairs with Roxanne.

But the damage had been done. It was clear that the others were not sure if Peggy had stolen the ring or not. Kitty avoided her for the rest of the day. Mrs Madden and Mrs O'Connor were cool towards her, speaking to her only to tell her what to do. By dinnertime they were ignoring her. Peggy felt shaky and near to tears. No one would believe her!

Kitty went off to bed early and did not offer to help with the washing up. There was a mountain of it to do – plates and dishes and all the pots and pans and roasting tins.

'They're all to be done tonight, Peggy,' ordered Mrs O'Connor as she left the kitchen and disappeared up to her room.

The tears Peggy had bottled up since that afternoon slid down her face. It isn't fair, she thought. Why don't they believe me? They've no proof I took it.

She wondered would she be dismissed for stealing. How would she ever get another job then? This time there could be no going back to Number 49. Peggy rolled up her sleeves.

The scullery was freezing but after an hour or so sweat dripped off her. Her hands were raw and her eyes stung. By the time she had finished it was one o'clock in the morning by the kitchen clock.

She tiptoed up the back stairs. She was exhausted and miserable. Kitty had turned on her side, facing away from her.

Peggy fell into bed in her uniform. She would have to get dressed in a few hours anyway. At least she would be ready to face the morning.

CHAPTER 20

Maids of All Work

THE NEXT MORNING PEGGY FELT totally drained and worn out. Kitty lay hunched and asleep in the other bed.

Sleep in, you weasel, see if I care! thought Peggy. She crept out of the room and busied herself downstairs. There was no sign of the other maid appearing.

Peggy could tell Mrs O'Connor was trying to avoid talking to her, but in the end she was forced to ask where Kitty was.

'If she's still asleep go up and wake her immediately, or the breakfasts will be late,' ordered the cook.

Peggy raced up the back stairs two at a time and pushed in the bedroom door.

'Kitty, are you awake yet?' Peggy looked across at Kitty. Her face was a greyish white and her breathing was shallow and rasping.

'Kitty, Kitty, are you feeling all right?'

'Peggy, get someone!' Kitty murmured softly.

Peggy felt scared. 'Don't worry, Kitty, I'll go down and get Mrs Madden.' Needles of guilt pricked her.

The other girl nodded. She could barely speak.

The housekeeper came to her door in a large white

nightdress and frilly nightcap. Peggy spoke so fast that Mrs Madden couldn't get the gist of it.

'Calm down, Peggy! What in heaven's name is it?'

'It's Kitty, she's really sick! You have to come. I don't know what's wrong with her.'

The housekeeper saw it was urgent and followed her back up to the attic room. She pushed Peggy aside and knelt down at Kitty's bed. She felt her forehead, then lifted her wrist and held it for a minute.

'Peggy, go down to the landing and fetch up two blankets for her. She's freezing. Get two spare pillows as well and we'll see if we can raise her up to get her to breathe more easily.'

Peggy was back in an instant, and the housekeeper issued further instructions.

'Tell Mrs O'Connor we want one of her special honey and lemon drinks, and you're to bring it straight up to Kitty before you make a start on the breakfast.'

Down in the kitchen Mrs O'Connor was still unforgiving. She made the drink and passed it in silence to Peggy.

'Don't dare dilly dally, Peggy, as you'll have to serve the breakfast.'

A few minutes later, Peggy was shaking with nervousness as she carried the heavy silver tray upstairs.

There were only two for breakfast, the Master and young Simon. The Master was engrossed, reading over some document, and Simon was busy making patterns with his scrambled egg.

The ladies did not ring for their breakfast until mid-morning and had it served on trays in their bedrooms. Peggy kept her eyes down and did not look either of them in the face. Neither seemed to notice that she had replaced Kitty.

Over the next few hours Peggy learned the difference between an upstairs and a downstairs maid.

'A maid of all work, that's what I am now!' she moaned, running to answer the bell yet again. Being upstairs gave her a chance every hour or so to pop up the extra flights of stairs to check on Kitty. She wasn't much better and barely touched the chicken broth and fresh bread Peggy had brought her for lunch. Peggy carried the tray back down to the kitchen.

That night Peggy fell into bed. Kitty had rolled over on her side to sleep.

'Are you any better, Kitty?'

The other girl didn't seem to have the energy to answer. Peggy felt sorry for Kitty, and decided that it was no use being angry with her anymore. She lay still in her own bed, looking at the wooden beams of the ceiling. A tiny spider was working away on a web. The draught kept blowing through the wood and knocking her off her perch. Undefeated, she'd jiggle back up her swinging life-line and begin again.

Not one person had had a kind word for Peggy all day. She closed her eyes. There's no point in feeling sorry for yourself, she thought. Tomorrow's another day.

The next day Mrs Madden requested that the Mistress call in the doctor for Kitty. He arrived mid-morning and Peggy was told to stay downstairs as Mrs Madden led him up to the attic bedroom.

Peggy paced up and down. Now she was very anxious about her friend. It wasn't until lunchtime, when she was sitting eating some leftover vegetable pie, that the housekeeper sat down beside her.

'Peggy, I know you're worried about Kitty. We all are. She has developed some type of infection in her chest which is affecting her lungs. She's very weak and will probably start to run a fever. The doctor has left a prescription which I'll get filled this afternoon. She's also to have plenty of fluids and be kept warm. She needs a hot flannel with turpentine poured on it placed on her chest to help her breathe – you can bring it up to her in a few minutes. She will need plenty of rest and someone to keep a good eye on her ...' Mrs Madden trailed off.

'I'll do it! All I care is that she gets better,' declared Peggy.

'Good girl, I knew I could rely on you.'

* * *

Roxanne still pestered Mrs Madden.

'That girl should be dismissed,' she demanded, pointing her finger at Peggy.

'You have most likely mislaid the ring, Miss Roxanne,' suggested Mrs Madden.

'Mislaid it! I certainly did not mislay it! I put it where she'd find it because I knew she'd keep it ...' Roxanne stopped, realising she had said too much.

Mrs Madden was shocked.

'That maid Peggy O'Driscoll is a troublemaker,' said Roxanne defiantly, 'and is not fit to work here.'

Mrs Madden stood up. 'There's no proof that Peggy did anything wrong, Miss Roxanne.'

Roxanne stormed out to the garden.

Mrs Madden went down to the kitchen where she and Mrs O'Connor had a heart-to-heart. Then they called Peggy in.

'Roxanne set you up, Peggy,' said Mrs Madden. 'It happens sometimes!'

'*Did* you see or touch the ring, Peggy?' asked the cook.

Peggy could only tell the truth. 'I found it in my duster all covered in dust from under the window seat. It was a nasty-looking thing so I stuck it in my pocket to give you, Mrs Madden.'

'Why didn't you say so, you silly girl,' groaned the housekeeper.

'But it was gone – it must have got lost. I put it in this pocket,' and she pulled out the pocket to show them.

Right where the seams joined a tiny split had opened. 'I forgot to sew it,' wailed Peggy, 'and the ring must have fallen out somewhere when I was cleaning.'

Shamefaced, both the housekeeper and the cook apologised for doubting her word. Peggy was so tired and fed up she just shrugged her shoulders and told them she was never one for grudges.

That evening Mrs Rowan discovered the ring near the bookshelves in the music room.

'So that little snake has her ring back,' muttered Mrs O'Connor. 'Keep out of her way, Peggy, in future.'

Over the next few days Peggy barely had time to notice what was going on around her. She ran all over the place trying to do Kitty's work and her own, raced up and down the stairs to check on the invalid, and every so often brought her drinks or emptied the chamber pot.

Kitty was so weak she could barely sit up and just

wanted to sleep all the time. She wouldn't eat a pick. Peggy's afternoon off came and went, and she was too busy to leave the house.

CHAPTER 21

Autumn Changes

THE FALL HAD ARRIVED. EVERY tree was changing colour and Greenbay had become a golden avenue. Although it continued to be sunny and warm, Peggy found it much easier to work. Kitty was still confined to bed.

The kitchen was a hive of activity as Mrs O'Connor was busy making preserves and chutneys from the abundance of fresh fruit and vegetables available. The smell of sugar and vinegar and pickling wafted around the house. The pantry shelves were bulging as if in preparation for a siege.

Mrs Madden surprised them all.

'I have some news to tell you.' Two spots of colour appeared on her cheeks. 'I'll be leaving Rushton at the end of the month.'

A large smile spread across her face. 'You're looking at the proprietor of The Haven, a new first-class lodging house in Walnut Hills at the far side of Greenbay. I'll be open for business in about five weeks' time and I hope eventually to have five or six guests.'

'Like Mrs Halligan's,' quipped Peggy.

'A bit more refined I should hope,' said Mrs Madden.

'My first lodger is a professor who has been widowed and wants to return to live in the area.'

Mrs O'Connor winked at Peggy who began to giggle. Mrs Madden, flustered and blushing, fled to the sanctuary of her room.

'God, isn't it great!' murmured Peggy, her spirit uplifted by Mrs Madden's single-minded achievement. She began to dream about her own future, Maybe one day she too ...

'No better woman deserves it,' said Mrs O'Connor. 'Sheila Madden has scrimped and scraped and worked hard and saved ever since she first set foot in this country. Her good-for-nothing husband grabbed and drank every penny they earned and then one day when the money ran out, so did he. He probably drank himself to death a long time back. I've worked with her for the last few years. We've had our differences but she has always had my respect and friendship.'

As the time for Mrs Madden to leave was drawing nearer, she called Peggy into her office. She handed her the usual brown envelope.

'Do you want to check it, Peggy?'

Peggy shook her head and smiled.

'You know, Peggy, you're very bright. Not that many in service can read and write, and obviously you're good with numbers too. I've spotted you scanning my rows of figures. Things are tough at the moment, but hard work, so they say, never killed anyone. Keep on working and I'm sure you'll go places. You've got brains and spirit and a good nature.'

Peggy nodded. 'Thank you. I wish you weren't going,' she told the older woman.

'I know, Peggy. But I've more than paid my dues, and this is what I've worked and saved for all these years. Now is my time to take a chance. You know, Walnut Hills isn't the end of the earth. It's only about an hour from here.' She stared at Peggy and the girl knew straight away that she would always have another friend.

'Now, before I get too sentimental, Mrs O'Connor and I were talking and we both agreed you must have a proper day off before I leave. You need a break from Rushton, so next Thursday, once you've served breakfast and helped prepare lunch, the rest of the day is yours.'

Later on Peggy was in the middle of sweeping the drawing-room floor and polishing the huge gilt mirror when Mrs Rowan came in.

'Oh, Peggy, there's a letter for you, all the way from Ireland.' She handed the simple white envelope over to Peggy.

Peggy wanted to open it there and then and find out about them all, but as the Mistress was watching her, she just popped it into the pocket of her apron and continued cleaning. She could feel it almost burning against her thigh and her blood was racing around her body in anticipation.

Finally, at midday, under the pretext of bringing a hot drink to Kitty, she ran all the way up to the top of the house. She placed the drink near the other maid's bed, and quiet as a mouse sat down on her own bed. She smelt the envelope. It seemed to smell of Ireland – damp and windy and beautiful. Inside there were two letters. The first was from Nano. Peggy could hardly stop herself from crying out loud.

> *My dearest grandniece, Peggy,*
>
> *It was with great joy and relief that Eily and I received your letter and the news of your safe arrival in Boston. You were always a strong little survivor. It is good to know that you are engaged in a fine position with a good family. To get a start straight away was a lucky thing and I know you will work hard as a Kitchen Maid.*
>
> *Eily and John got married. Your sister never looked so beautiful or John so handsome. It was a small wedding. How I wished you and your parents had been here to see it. Michael got time off.*
>
> *The shop closed down about two weeks after. It near broke my heart. Every time we pass through Castletaggart we see it boarded up and empty.*
>
> *Now we are all living on the farm. Joshua Powers and I get on very well and he is glad to have company around the place again.*
>
> *You know it reminds me of my childhood to be surrounded by the open fields and the animals.*
>
> *There isn't a night I don't think of you and say a prayer for you.*
>
> *God keep you safe.*
> *With love and affection,*
>
> *Nano*

The second letter was written in Eily's large round letters.

My dear little sister,

I miss you so much. The place is empty without your laughter.

John and I are so happy. Powers Farm is such a special place for me. Do you remember when we were little girls in Duneen? That is the happiness I feel here.

Michael is well and is now let ride out two of the horses. John is busy bringing in hay and doing jobs getting ready for the winter.

Nano cried for two days after we left the shop. But Joshua asked her to help him with a young calf that had lost its mother and since then they have become good friends.

I miss the shop at times but am kept busy housekeeping here. Oh Peggy, I must tell you – I think I might be with child. It is very early to tell, but Nano says I have a broody look about me. Say a prayer that all goes well.

I miss you. I miss you. I miss you.
Do you like America?
Write back as soon as you get a chance.

All my love
Your fond sister,

Eily

Peggy held the two letters up to her chest. The tears were streaming down her face. While she was reading she could picture Eily in the small farm kitchen, baking soda bread. She could almost smell the fire and the bread. She sobbed out loud.

Kitty stirred and woke up.

'Peggy, what is it, are you sick?' The other girl's voice was full of concern. 'Why are you crying?'

Peggy sniffed and rubbed the palms of her hands to her eyes.

'I don't know if I'm crying with sadness or happiness to tell the truth. It's just I miss them all so much. Here, Kitty, take this drink I brought up.' She hugged her friend and helped her to sit up in bed. That way Kitty could look out the window and see the garden and a bit of the roadway.

'Peggy, you're so lucky! I never got a letter from anyone – anyways, what good would it do me since I couldn't even read it.' The other girl was smiling a wobbly smile.

'I'd better get back down,' moaned Peggy. Then she brightened up. 'Did I tell you I'm going to be an auntie?'

* * *

On Thursday Peggy felt her heart dance as the heavy gate clicked shut behind her. Kitty had told her the name of some good secondhand shops and had given her two dollars for a list of small items she needed.

On reaching Boston she knew the first place she wanted to go to. She walked up towards the corner of Empire Hill. The same portraits were still in the window of the daguerreotype studio. As she pushed in the door, a tall thin bespectacled man came forward to greet her.

Peggy introduced herself and explained what she wanted.

'A wise decision, Miss O'Driscoll.'

He explained the prices and the different types of portrait available. Peggy settled on the most basic model and on two copies.

'Do you want a costume or not?' he enquired, pointing to a rail of clothes to one side. She walked over to the rail and looked at what was on offer. There was a nasty-looking fox-fur stole. Two or three patterned silk blouses. There was a vivid red satin evening shawl. She tried on a dark green coat with velvet around the collar. There was a small bonnet to go with it. She stared at her reflection. She looked older and paler, but no, it wasn't her. Eily and Nano were not ones to have the wool pulled over their eyes. Her uniform would have to do. She put the things back and stood against the cream-painted background. A tall thin vase of flowers stood on a carved wooden pedestal near her.

The man stepped back and seated himself behind a strange-looking box. He slid another box inside it. There was a burning acid smell.

'Try and stay fairly still, Miss O'Driscoll, as I'm trying to focus on you.'

Peggy tried to fix a smile on her face though there was no denying she was feeling a bit nervous.

It seemed to take an age before she was finished. She paid Mr Marvin Aubert half the money due – the rest she would pay when she collected the daguerreotype plates on her next day off. She almost skipped down the street. Just think what Eily and Nano would say when they saw the picture of her. Leastways, they would never forget what she looked like! She found the general store and got the things Kitty needed. Then she made for the secondhand shop.

There was a smell of mustiness but nothing a breath of fresh air wouldn't chase away. Within half an hour it seemed as if she had tried on nearly every coat and wrap in the place. Some were much too big. Others had moth holes. A few needed major alterations which Peggy knew she would never manage and then, just when she had almost given up hope, she found the perfect coat. It was a rich purple, like the heather on the hills around Castletaggart. It was all made of wool and part-lined with a fine flannel inside. It had wide caped shoulders. The minute she slipped it on, it felt comfortable and cosy.

'I'll take it,' she announced to the surprised assistant who was sure she had no intention of buying.

'Don't bother wrapping it, I'll wear it,' she told her.

Outside there was a noticeable drop in temperature and Peggy thanked her lucky stars for the coat as she had to walk nearly half the way home.

CHAPTER 22

The New Housekeeper

ON SUNDAY MORNING SHEILA Madden said her final goodbyes to them all. The night before there had been a special dinner cooked by Mrs O'Connor, and the Rowan family had come down to the kitchen to toast the housekeeper and present her with a gift.

'Open it! Open it!' shouted Simon.

Blushing, Mrs Madden had opened the large box to reveal a glass decanter and six glasses. 'I'll treasure them always,' she said.

From Mrs O'Connor there was an apron and a recipe holder.

'You might have need to do a bit of cooking yourself now,' she joked.

Peggy watched as the housekeeper opened her gift. It was a small paperweight, a sea-blue colour. On top of it was written: For the Lady of the House.

'Peggy, thank you! It's just perfect.'

Before she left, Mrs Madden went up the stairs to the
attic room. Kitty was sitting up in bed now. She looked
wan and pasty and her hair was greasy. Peggy had
plaited it and tied it back.

Kitty handed over her gift. Mrs Madden hugged her
close and then tearfully opened the package that Peggy
had got for Kitty. It was a pair of fine gardening gloves,
just like the ones the Mistress wore.

'For your own garden,' smiled Kitty.

Peggy helped the housekeeper carry down her
baggage. Her simple room looked bare as they went
downstairs.

Mr Rowan was sitting impatiently in the driveway
and Simon was running in and out, annoying the horse.
Peggy helped to store the bags and case under the seats.
Mrs Madden stepped up.

'I'll run down to the kitchen gate to watch as you go,'
shouted Peggy.

As the horse and carriage passed on its way about two
minutes later, she noticed that the housekeeper never
turned round – not even once.

* * *

Two days later Miss Hannah Lewis, the new
housekeeper, arrived. She was unmarried and by
every-one's reckoning around the fifty mark. She
was a second cousin of Mr Rowan's and had decided
to accept the recently vacated post of housekeeper.
She was small and mean and definitely 'in charge', as
they all found out soon enough.

She was given a free hand by Mrs Rowan, who realised

that without the likes of Mrs Madden to supervise the worry of the house she could never manage.

'I'm a simple God-fearing woman,' announced Miss Lewis, 'and I'll not tolerate laziness or waste. My first duty is a full inspection of the kitchen.' She made Mrs O'Connor follow her round as she opened doors and examined cooking equipment and delftware, taking a full inventory of every piece, down to the last teaspoon. Peggy, who was busy trying to finish off the ironing, had just come down with a fresh load of tablecloths and some traycloths. The air in the kitchen was tense. Once Miss Lewis left to check the linen, Mrs O'Connor launched into a tirade against the new housekeeper.

'Let that old rip say one word about my cooking and I'll get my hat and coat and go and find a better position.'

Peggy, wide-eyed, knew that she meant it. Hearing the bell clang, Peggy ran up the stairs where Miss Lewis asked her to explain the stock-taking system and notebook kept by Mrs Madden.

'It may need some re-organisation when I get a chance,' Miss Lewis informed her. 'Are you the only maid in the house?' she asked.

'No, there's Kitty too, but she's been sick.'

'Where is she?'

'She's upstairs in our room.'

'I want to see her straight away!'

Peggy led the way upstairs. Passing the housekeeper's room Miss Lewis wagged her finger.

'I'll be able to keep a good eye and ear on you both.'

They trudged up the smaller stairs. Peggy coughed loudly a few times, hoping to alert her friend to the fact that they had a visitor. Miss Lewis led the way into the

room. Kitty immediately sat up. Her hair looked filthy
and tangled and she was still half-asleep. The room
was stuffy and a mess of blankets, patchwork bed-
spread and underclothes lay in a heap on the floor. The
housekeeper's face was tight and strained.

'This is a disgrace! Open that window and let in some
air. You are like two animals living in a cave. I will not
have it in my household.'

Peggy tried to explain about having to do the breakfasts on her own and make the beds and the ironing and
that she'd hoped to get back up after lunch and tidy the
place. Miss Lewis would not listen. She pointed to the
full chamber pot.

'Empty that! Immediately!'

Peggy began to make her way down the back stairs.
There was a servants' water closet outside near the
woodshed.

When Peggy returned Miss Lewis had departed.
Kitty's eyes were red-rimmed.

'She says I'm under notice, unless I get better soon.'

Peggy stood still. She didn't know what to say or do.
Miss Lewis now ruled the roost and the maids were her
last concern.

* * *

The next day Peggy was dusting and cleaning Roxanne's
room. The bedroom was filled with so many fine things
that Peggy couldn't help but envy her. On the bedside table
lay a brown leather-covered book. Peggy held it while she
polished the side table with beeswax. She loved the smell of
polish and always liked to see a room shining as she left it.

'What have got in your hand?'

Peggy was surprised by Roxanne's arrival. She thought she was in the middle of a piano lesson downstairs. Without thinking, Peggy looked at the title of the book.

'It's *Uncle Tom's Cabin,* by Harriet Beecher Stowe. It's a grand story, Miss Roxanne.'

'You've read it, I suppose?' said Roxanne sarcastically.

'Yes, Miss Roxanne. It was serialised in the newspaper. Kitty and I loved it.'

'Do you think I would read a book that skivvies like you would read – two stupid Bridgets from the bogs?'

Peggy could feel her blood boil. She placed the book back on the table and bent to get her cleaning box. As she stood up she couldn't resist saying: 'I do believe your President and Queen Victoria are both admirers of Mrs Beecher Stowe's story – but it may not be your cup of tea!'

She was just at the doorway when she felt a sudden blow. The heavy book hit the side of her head and then her shoulder.

Peggy managed to steady herself by holding onto the door handle. A dazed feeling washed over her. Standing on the wide landing, she could hear Roxanne laughing. Miss Lewis came out of the bathroom when she heard the clatter.

'If you've broken something, Peggy, it will be docked from your wages. I've told you that before.'

Peggy leant against the panelling. Her head was aching. She put her hand up and felt a trickle of blood running down through her hair and over her right eye.

'Miss Roxanne flung a book at me – she's a bad-tempered weasel!'

The woman stared at her. 'Hold your tongue, girl. Don't you dare complain about your betters!'

'But it's not fair, I did nothing. Just because …'

'Don't say one more word. I will not have the likes of you answering back and causing trouble.'

Peggy sniffed. She waited to see if the housekeeper would stand up for her. But Hannah Lewis's eyes were cold and unflinching. She did not care a toss what happened to the young maid.

'Clean up that cut and then attend to your duties.'

Peggy went downstairs. Mrs O'Connor made a great fuss over her and told her to sit down and have a cup of tea and get her wind back. Later on, as she washed the roasting tin and scrubbed at the greasy pans, Peggy felt tears forcing their way out. Every time she moved her shoulder it hurt and by tomorrow no doubt it would be black and blue. As she looked out through the barred scullery window all she could see were the bare branches of the trees above. The garden was sleeping. All the blooms had been picked. The air was chill and a cold wind blew. There wasn't even a weed to be seen.

CHAPTER 23

Mutiny

ALMOST AS SOON AS THE NEW housekeeper arrived there were changes at Rushton. Miss Lewis insisted that she go through the family menu with the Mistress. This meant that Mrs O'Connor lost daily contact with the lady of the house and got no chance to air her grievances. Miss Lewis also ordered that only basic simple food should be provided downstairs. As far as Peggy and Mrs O'Connor could see, this meant cuts of the worst meat and offal.

'Tripe and liver and God knows what. Most of this stuff isn't fit for a dog!' moaned the cook.

'Well, not Bonaparte anyways,' joked Peggy.

'That creature is better fed than ourselves! 'Tis only the best for him – none of this rubbish.' Mrs O'Connor cast a despairing glance at an offending dish of tripe which was beginning to smell. Peggy, who had usually filled up with thick slices of crusty vegetable-and-meat pies, found that she was often hungry now. Slices of cake and the upstairs pudding were off limits. A basic rice or tapioca pudding or a bread- and-butter pudding made from stale bread were adequate. However, Miss Lewis felt that as a second cousin of the family, she herself should enjoy the same menu as the Rowans.

'I'll guarantee the quality of the food. I'm sure I'll eat with the family at times, but mostly I prefer the solitude of my room and the company of the Good Book,' she asserted.

Mrs O'Connor nightly carried in the plate of delicious food and banged it down in front of her.

The cook worked with skill, but often nothing could disguise the greasiness of the aged mutton or hashed beef that they had to eat. Peggy longed for the rich steak-and-kidney pies and the delicious roast pork of Mrs Madden's day. As she worked, her stomach groaned and grumbled and sometimes a weakness came over her.

There were words in the kitchen when Miss Lewis discovered Mrs O'Connor reading out loud from the papers. She told the cook there was to be no 'scandal-mongery' in the kitchen of Rushton! Miss Lewis would read a chapter of the Bible if they needed to listen to something.

Miss Lewis also insisted that Kitty attend to the mending and darning of the household since she was now well enough to sit up. 'Everyone here must earn their keep,' she announced. But the large basket of mending often lay untouched on the floor next to Kitty's bed. 'If that girl isn't back on her feet again soon, she'll definitely go!' said the housekeeper.

Mrs O'Connor was afraid for the young maid. Every day she whipped up two whole eggs with a tiny drop of sherry and sent Peggy quick as lightning up the stairs with it to the invalid to try and build her up again. Peggy had strict instructions to make sure the other maid drank every bit of it and not to let 'that old one' catch her.

Not a day went by without the new housekeeper making some comment about Kitty.

'Is that girl getting any better?'

Peggy would keep her head down and carry on working.

'I'll have to get her moved to an infirmary or women's shelter.'

Peggy listened, hoping her thumping heart could not be heard.

'Didn't you hear me, Peggy? It's not fair on you. How can you manage doing the work of two? We really need to get a replacement as soon as possible.'

Peggy and Mrs O'Connor knew that Kitty must show signs of recovery if she was to save herself from being dismissed. They were both fond of her, and knew she was too weak to survive on her own.

As soon as the housekeeper disappeared for a few hours they went up and brought Kitty downstairs. She was washed and cleaned and then she sat at the fire with the cook while Peggy cleared out the attic room and re-made the bed.

After a while Kitty was able to help Mrs O'Connor prepare the afternoon tea and gradually she got back on her feet. Peggy always made sure to do the heavy work and if Miss Lewis tried to force Kitty to do some task that would be too much for her, Mrs O'Connor would find some urgent job in the kitchen that needed doing.

Once or twice Mrs Rowan came downstairs. She stood in the centre of the kitchen, looking totally out of place.

'I know you must all miss Mrs Madden, but Miss Lewis is a very experienced housekeeper. Her last position was in an Academy for Young Ladies. My husband is very pleased as she is able to talk to him about the economies she has made in the household budget. I've no head for figures, but no doubt it is all being well handled.'

Peggy and Kitty shifted uneasily. Mrs O'Connor was stirring a basin of cake mixture, grim and silent.

'We'll see about that,' she muttered fiercely as the Mistress swept out of the kitchen.

Over the next few days a sense of mutiny took hold in the kitchen. There was silence when Miss Lewis entered, or else Mrs O'Connor would noisily sing a verse of some hymn. The other woman would purse her lips and walk by.

It was curious, but every second day some member of the family seemed to find a lump of gristle or piece of bone in their meal. One evening the Master nearly choked on a piece of fish-bone hidden under an Italian sauce.

Later they heard him talking to his cousin in her room where she was just finishing off her own dinner.

'Damnation, woman, I'll not have second-rate food in my own home.'

'But Gregory, this is the finest quality fish. That stupid cook mustn't have cleaned it or cut it up properly.'

Once the Master left her room, Hannah Lewis made straight for the kitchen. Mrs O'Connor was sitting in the chair near the fire, looking at yesterday's paper.

'You are deliberately trying to fight my authority and I will not have it. I am in charge of running the household, Mrs O'Connor. If you cannot take proper care in the preparation of food, well, I'm sure you can guess the outcome. I'll say no more.' And turning around she marched back to her room and banged the door.

Mrs O'Connor shook the paper. 'The old bag! But we'll never get the better of her.'

CHAPTER 24

Good Riddance

PEGGY WAS EXHAUSTED WAXing and re-waxing the floor of the landing. Miss Lewis had made her re-do the polishing three times before it was to her satisfaction. Today was Mrs O'Connor's day off. She left the house at one o'clock and told them not to expect her back till late. Peggy and Kitty both suspected she was looking for another position. Peggy knew she would have to spend the afternoon in the kitchen helping the housekeeper prepare the evening meal.

'Any housekeeper worth her salt should be able to turn her hand to everything. I'm a fine cook, even if I do say it myself,' Miss Lewis announced smugly.

Peggy noted that the menu was more lavish than usual and she knew that the housekeeper was trying to show Mrs O'Connor up. For the main course there would be beef with oysters, and a fig pudding and a lemon cheesecake for dessert.

Although it was freezing outside, the walls of the kitchen were damp with heat.

'Peggy, go out and get me some fresh parsley and assorted herbs,' Miss Lewis ordered.

'But it's freezing and starting to get dark,' Peggy reminded her.

'Just do as you're told!'

Peggy had no time to go up and get her shawl. Luckily an old scarf of Mrs O'Connor's hung near the back door and she wrapped it round herself. It was bitter outside after the heat of the kitchen. The ground was already beginning to harden and get frosty.

She snipped some parsley and lemon balm and sage and mace. Most of the plants had died back for the winter and Mrs O'Connor kept a supply of dried herbs in the kitchen – but oh no! that wasn't good enough for Miss Lewis.

Peggy was just about to get up and go back to the warm kitchen when she noticed a strange herb close to the earth, meandering under the lavender bush. It looked like green-eye. Yes, she recognised it. Auntie Nano was always one for teaching you all about plants and herbs. Nano always swore that one little leaf of the green-eye was the best cure for anyone whose stomach had got frozen up and was constipated – one leaf was enough to get things moving! Peggy picked a tiny bunch of the herb and put it in her pocket.

Although she had started to shiver and her teeth were chattering, Peggy almost felt like whistling as she went back into the kitchen.

'Wash the parsley and herbs and bring them over to me.'

'Of course, Miss Lewis,' she replied.

The housekeeper chopped the herbs finely and left them on the chopping board. 'I'll just sprinkle them on the meat once we're ready to serve. Good for the blood, you know!'

While the housekeeper was pouring the soup into the tureen, Peggy added the green-eye which she had chopped to the rest of the herbs. The housekeeper then began to lay the tender fillets of beef with the oysters artistically on the plates. With her fingers she sprinkled a dusting of herbs across her handiwork.

'Miss Roxanne only likes the leanest cut of meat, but I know she loves parsley,' Peggy couldn't resist saying, and she noticed with glee the two sprinklings the cook gave that portion. 'Master Simon likes his meat plain,' added Peggy guiltily, but still a hint of the garnish dusted his smaller portion.

An innocent Kitty carried up the serving tray. There was a left-over mutton stew for them, but Peggy had never enjoyed anything like it. Miss Lewis sat at the far end of the kitchen table. She had an extra helping of oysters for herself and emptied all that was left on the chopping board over her plate.

Peggy disappeared into the scullery to do the washing up early. Kitty was serving the fig pudding and lemon cheesecake.

Soon the kitchen gleamed and everything was in its place. There was no point in hanging around downstairs as Mrs O'Connor was still out. Kitty and Peggy were glad of an early night and the chance to do some reading, which they had been neglecting. Peggy decided not to tell Kitty what she had done because it would only implicate the other girl if she was found out, and she knew how afraid and weak Kitty was in that kind of situation.

At about midnight there were strange sounds from the room below. The housekeeper seemed to be knocking on the walls.

Kitty and Peggy both woke up with a start.

'Do you think she's calling us?' wondered Kitty.

Peggy was still half-asleep. 'No, she'd come and get us if she wanted us.'

Once they were awake they became aware of the constant flushing of the water closet on the floor below. Suddenly Mrs O'Connor appeared at the door, still wearing her coat and hat.

'For God's sake, girls, get up and give us a hand. The whole house is in an uproar. They're all sick, with pains in their stomachs and running to the toilet all night. I've never seen the like of it.'

Peggy and Kitty had never seen the like of it either! They ferried hot drinks, stomach remedies and fresh linen back and forth all night. Even Bonaparte, who had been fed on Roxanne's leftovers, was barking all the time to be let out to the garden. With pleasure Peggy opened the front door and let him off. Hearing his wails and moans, Peggy found it difficult to stop laughing. A twinge of guilt did strike her as she read a story to Master Simon to get him back to sleep. He was pale but his eyes were drowsy and in no time he snuggled back under the blankets and slept for the night.

The next morning Peggy and Kitty went straight down to the kitchen. They had their breakfast with Mrs O'Connor. There would be no need to bother cooking a breakfast as the whole family were still sleeping and would be lucky to manage a cup of weak tea. Peggy and Kitty had heard a combination of moans and snoring as they passed outside the housekeeper's door.

Peggy was bent double in stitches, until she saw the

confused look in the other maid's eyes.

'Well, girls, I tell you I've never seen the like of it. If you ask me they've been poisoned. 'Twas something they ate. I tell you, that old rat bag couldn't cook an egg!' And the cook gave them an extra egg each.

Later, Kitty was sent to the doctor's house to request an urgent visit to Rushton. When he arrived he was led from one bedroom to the next, examining each of the patients separately. Simon was clearly feeling better as he was jumping up and down on the bed.

The doctor came down the hallway to Mrs O'Connor. She led him in the direction of the housekeeper's room. A few minutes later he went back to talk to the Master who was too ill to even consider going to his office despite having a series of meetings arranged.

'It would seem to be some kind of gastric poisoning,' announced Doctor Chapman. 'Mrs O'Connor, I'll leave the five invalids in your good care. Plenty of fluids – broth, beef tea and the like – and a light diet for the next two or three days. If by any chance there's a turn for the worse,' he glanced knowingly at the cook, 'you should call me again.'

A look of alarm spread across the cook's face.

'Worse! God almighty, how could the five of them be worse than they are already? Tell me that!' she muttered, making her way back down to the kitchen.

Doctor Chapman made a mental note as he stepped into his pony and trap never under any circumstances to mix oysters with fig pudding.

Two days later, the Master sent for both the cook and the housekeeper to come to his study. Two sets of raised voices could be heard from the room. After the meeting

Hannah Lewis came out, her eyes blazing, but her face pale and tired-looking. She was defeated. Mrs O'Connor reigned supreme and the Master had agreed that she would have a say in the appointment of the next new housekeeper.

'We have all learned a lesson,' said the Master grimly.

'Let's hope they remember it,' joked Mrs O'Connor later on as the servants ate their lunch.

Within two hours the other woman had packed her belongings and departed from the house.

'Goodbye and good riddance,' declared the cook.

CHAPTER 25

Thanksgiving

NEAR THE END OF NOVEMBER the weather turned bitterly cold. Every morning when they woke, Peggy and Kitty had to crack the ice in the water jug to wash. Blue-nosed and shivering they dragged on their warm uniforms and fled to the heat of the kitchen.

The whole place was in turmoil, preparing for Thanksgiving.

'But what is Thanksgiving?' asked Peggy.

'It's a kind of feastday – a holiday I suppose,' answered Kitty vaguely. 'Anyways, 'tis fierce important.'

Whatever it was it meant a mountain of work as there would be lots of cousins coming to stay at Rushton. The house had to be cleaned from top to bottom until it glowed. Mrs O'Connor was all het up in the kitchen with the amount of cooking to be done.

Every time Peggy went down to the woodshed to fetch logs, the glassy stare of the enormous turkey swinging upside down from a meat-hook greeted her. Its ugly face and beak and dead body brushed against her as she went in and out. 'God, it's terrible,' she said.

Mrs O'Connor handed Peggy a large, strange-looking object.

'Now, Peggy, scoop out the flesh and chop it up,' she ordered.

'What kind of a thing is this, Mrs O'Connor?'

'It's a pumpkin, child, for pumpkin pie,' said the cook, laughing.

Peggy stared at the great orange vegetable on the chopping board. Its bright flesh was full of flattish pips and there was a strange smell from it. Heaven knows what kind of pie you'd get from it!

Although they were very busy there was a sense of peace in the kitchen. In two weeks' time a new house-keeper would start, but for now they were on their own.

'Any more word from home, Peggy?' asked the cook.

'No, but I sent them the picture of myself and a bit of savings. It'll help towards the cost of the baby and getting the house done up. I want them to know I'm all right, that I'm set up.'

Mrs O'Connor laughed. 'Aren't you the great one. Sure, they'll be right proud of you. You'll go far, Peggy.'

The next day was Thanksgiving. The smell of roasting turkey filled the house and the dining-table was sparkling with shining crystal, fine china and silver. Peggy watched from the stairs as the family and their guests filed into the dining-room. She had expected the Mistress, Roxanne and the rest of them to be dressed in their best finery, but was amazed to see them in simple, plain clothes.

'It's in honour of times past and their pilgrim ancestors,' whispered Mrs O'Connor.

It took the two of them to lift the magnificent roasted

bird out of the oven, place it on the giant platter and then carry it upstairs. Kitty served the sweet potatoes and buttered corn. The Master began to carve the turkey to the cheers of all at the table.

An hour later Peggy and the others in the kitchen were sitting down to their own Thanksgiving dinner.

'No turkey ever tasted better,' declared Kitty, smiling at the cook.

Peggy loved the crisp golden skin and the unusual taste of the meat, and the bittersweet cranberries. She was a bit suspicious of the pumpkin pie, but it too was delicious. She was getting used to strange tastes and new things, and this was the finest meal she had eaten since leaving Castletaggart.

Thinking about home, she fingered the horsehair circle Michael had made for her. It hung from a ribbon round her neck now, inside her uniform. Ireland, Eily, Michael and Nano – nothing would ever take their memory away or make her forget them. But still there was so much she could do here in America. Sure she had to work hard for every dollar she earned, but by heaven she had plans for those dollars. In only half a year her life had changed so much. Yet with all that had happened – the fear, the hardships, the homesickness – she had survived.

'Peggy! You're daydreaming again,' joked Kitty.

Peggy looked around. It was strange, but sitting here in the kitchen at Rushton, celebrating her first American Thanksgiving, she felt at home. Kitty and Mrs O'Connor had almost become her family. She thought about Sarah, and hoped she too was happy. She was to meet her on her next Sunday afternoon off, when Sarah and her brothers would have a small celebration of their own.

The bell from upstairs rang.

'Oh, no,' moaned Kitty, 'what do they want now?'

Peggy hopped up. 'You stay. I'll get it.'

She got up from the table and ran off up the stairs.

The *Children of the Famine* Trilogy

UNDER THE HAWTHORN TREE
Ireland in the 1840s is devastated by famine. When tragedy strikes their family, Eily, Michael and Peggy are left to fend for themselves. Starving and in danger of being sent to the workhouse, they escape. Their only hope is to find the great-aunts they have heard about in their mother's stories. With tremendous courage, they set out on a journey that will test every reserve of strength, love and loyalty they possess.

FIELDS OF HOME
Only a few years ago, Eily, Michael and Peggy survived the Great Famine. Now Peggy is in America, hoping for a new life, and finally she heads for the Wild West. Eily and Michael face new challenges at home. Everywhere there is unrest, with evictions, burnings, secret meetings. What will become of them and of Eily's little girl, Mary-Brigid?

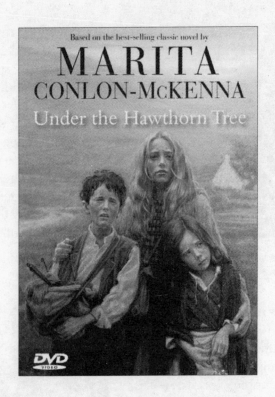